Guilty Desires
Sexy
Stories
Collection

VOLUME 8

12 EROTIC SHORT STORIES

TENA SELDAN

Publisher's Note: This is a work of fiction. Names,
characters, places, and incidents are a product of
the author's imagination. Locales and public
names are sometimes used for atmospheric
purposes. Any resemblance to actual people, living
or dead, or to businesses, companies, events,
institutions, or locales is completely coincidental.

Guilty Desires/ Tena Seldan. -- 1st ed.
Xplicit Press, an imprint of TLM Media LLC

ISBN-13: 978-1-62327-540-2
ISBN-10: 1623275407
eISBN: 978-1-62327-589-1

Printed in the United States of America

CONTENTS

1 CAN I DANCE FOR YOU?

Preface

The alarm clock on Starr's bedside table began to ring, reminding Starr of the busy weekend ahead of her. Starr let out a groan and threw her pillow over her face, wishing for just 10 more minutes of much needed beauty sleep. If people only realized what was involved in the job of being one of Los Angeles' top strippers, they would give her and her fellow strippers a bit more respect out in society. Of course, now that Starr was one of the top names in the country, she made mega bucks, but it hadn't always been that way. She literally danced her buns off, to the top. People were under the impression that strippers were just paid whores, but it simply wasn't the truth. Starr had the sore muscles to prove it.

Starr finally got out of bed, showered, and put on her yoga pants and tank top. She combed out her hip length, flaxen blonde hair, and let it dry naturally. Starr Ranes was absolutely stunning. There was no question about that. It was also no mystery, to anyone that had ever laid eyes on Starr, that she was made to be in the limelight.

Starr was one of LA's highest paid strippers at the prestigious LA strip club, known as the Silver Chalice. Starr didn't even have to make up some fake stripper name. She was born to hippie parents who named her Starr Light Ranes.

From the second she breathed her first breath on the earth, Starr had been absolutely beautiful. She had natural flaxen blonde hair and pale blue eyes. They looked as pale as the sky on a clear day. They looked almost like blue crystals.

But the most amazing thing that set Starr apart from other girls like her was her nature and personality. Starr was a sweetheart and very smart. Starr had never met a stranger and, as far as she knew, she didn't have any enemies –oh, unless you count Ebony Faytal at the club, who absolutely hated Starr for no apparent reason.

Starr had grown up in LA and was familiar with the area. Her best friend since junior high, was still her best friend. She was not a stripper at all. She was a cute brunette with short, pixie hair and a curvy body to die for. Her name was Robin.

She and Starr were closer than sisters. Robin was supposed to be there, any minute, to help motivate Starr to do her yoga and strength training. Starr had one of the most daring and impressive acts at the Silver Chalice, and she had to stay in tip top shape to perform it 4 nights a week.

Starr heard a tap on the door and she knew it was Robin. "Come on in, it's open," hollered Starr, from her gym. "Hey girlfriend, how's it going?" said Robin, as she bebopped through the door, shaking her bubble butt in her super short booty shorts. "How's my girl in her teensy booty shorts?" giggled Starr, who blew her best bud a kiss from the weight bench. "Cute Starr! You know, at least I wear clothes!" She ribbed her friend all in good fun.

"Damn, I'm sore! I hope I can keep up on the pole tonight. We are having three successive bachelor parties in a row!" said Starr. "It will be with some of LA's top business guys, and these dudes go wild when they party, let me tell you."

"Climb up on that pole girlfriend and I'll get your show girl music going. You show them what you got, okay?"

Starr was amazing on the pole. She could nearly fly, when she got going good. She could swing around lavishly, just holding on by her ankles, and her blonde hair blowing in the breeze. She was a definite pro and the best around. She had never fallen or even came close, and it took great skill to do what she did. After Starr felt as though she had warmed up enough, she got down from her pole and, she and Robin, had tuna sandwiches for lunch.

"So, are you going to come by the club tonight and cheer me on?" asked Starr.

"I'll try, bestie! Really, I will. I hope I get off in time to see my best friend knock them dead!"

Starr took a nap and got up, around 5, to get ready to go to work at the Silver Chalice, around 7. She put on her costume, under her warm ups. Tonight, she brought out one of her glitziest numbers, to start her show with. Five dancers usually alternated between the stages and, sometimes, up to 7. Usually, Starr had five or more shows in one given night.

Starr arrived at the Silver Chalice, at about 6:15, and started getting ready with her final touches in the dressing room. In the dressing room, she ran across Ebony Faytal. She was a Mexican dancer that was as mean as a junkyard dog and was jealous of Starr.

"Hi Starr, how many clients are you planning to hoard for yourself tonight?" said the hateful Ebony.

"Ebony, please, just put a lid on it. I am in no mood," said Starr. Just around that time, her best dancer gal pal walked in, looking all tired and worn out.

Her name was Cherry Lane and she was an adorable, strawberry blonde, with a petite little body that drove the guys wild. She ran up to Starr and threw her arms around her. "Oh Starr, Jake is at it, again! The motherfucker is cheating, again. He has a hot stripper for a girlfriend, for God's sake, what more does he want?" asked Cherry.

"I know sweetheart. He is missing out not you," Starr said. "Now, you get that little red pair of hot pants on and go stun those fellows, okay?"

Starr did the finishing touches on her makeup and put on her silver bikini bottoms, and silver glittery halter top, and her, come fuck me, silver go-go boots. Her long, blonde hair was pulled back, in a braid that she would be loosening in her show, later.

At straight up seven, the Silver Chalice was wall to wall with people, rocking and rolling. Starr was ready to start her show. She was just about ready for Bianca, the announcer, to introduce her. "Welcome, ladies and gentleman, to LA's most exotic show club in the entire state, with the most beautiful dancers you have ever seen! Performing for you, now, on the main stage, with her amazing routine, is Starr Ranes!" The crowd let out a loud roar and applause, and Starr came out, onstage, doing what she does best. She was on fire doing gymnastics, along with dirty dancing and the most amazing pole work anyone had ever seen. She had dollars flying out of her bottoms and top. As Starr was belly dancing, in front of the stage she saw a man that seemed mesmerized by her. Sure, she was used to that, but this guy seemed different, somehow.

He would not take his eyes off of Starr, as she did her pole routine. She slid and flipped, and wowed the audience with her skills. Once she finished her striptease act, she took requests for private shows and dances.

She noticed a man she didn't recognize wanted a private show. It was the same guy who was so vehemently watching her while she was pole dancing. "What the heck!" she thought. I may as well give him a show!

Starr entered the private area, where she did her dances, and there he sat. He was very handsome, she must admit. "Hello, beautiful Starr, I thoroughly enjoyed your performance. You stand out among the rest."

"Thank you, very much," she said.

"My name is Gregory Taylor, but you can call me Greg." He said, looking at her very sexily.

"Okay, Greg, what can I do for you this evening?" asked Starr, with her beautiful blue eyes dancing off of the candlelight.

"Can I just gaze at your dazzling beauty for a while?" he said.

"I guess so, but time is money, you know. But, I suppose it is your money and you can do with it what you want," Starr replied.

"How did you ever learn to do such amazing stunts on that pole?" asked Greg.

"Tons of practice, I suppose," said Starr. "So, are you ready for your private dance?" asked Starr.

"If you insist," said Greg, who was completely enamored, just looking at this beautiful goddess.

Starr began to move her beautiful body very seductively, swerving her hips in a grinding motion, all over Greg's body, daring him to become hard and tempted. She turned, with her back to him, and did a bump and grind motion over his legs, as if to say, fuck me now! Greg watched, as her perfect tush bounced up and down. He felt her pussy lips grazing his knee. She, then, turned to face him and shook her tits, right up in his face. Damn, she smelled good enough to eat! thought Greg.

He wanted to grab her and pull her in, close to him, so fucking bad. But he knew he couldn't do that here, or some burly bouncer would have him thrown out, on his ear.

Greg had been coming to strip clubs for years, but he had never seen a more beautiful and desirable dancer than Starr Ranes. As she danced and swirled in front of him, his cock became like steel in his pants. Greg motioned for Starr to come closer, so that he could ask her a question.

Starr walked toward him and said, "Yes, did you need something?"

"Yes, you are so, damn, beautiful and sexy, and you are making my cock grow very large! It is quite uncomfortable in my pants. Would it be awful of me to ask if I could watch you and beat my cock off?"

Starr couldn't help but smile and be a tiny bit flattered. He said it so sincerely and it secretly turned her on. "Sure baby! Jerk that dick off and watch me writhe in front of you," she said.

Starr didn't usually react in such an easy-going, open manner, but this guy was simply someone she could not resist.

Greg was a gorgeous guy. Of that, there was no doubt. He, too, was a blonde, and he had boyish good looks that had broken many hearts. He had that all American boy look that drove girls wild. His hair was a sun-washed blonde, and he had emerald green eyes that absolutely sparkled. Greg was also one of the hottest young attorneys in LA and was a hot commodity, as a bachelor. His eyes were nearly flames at this moment, as Starr performed her seductive moves for him, personally. The way she moved her hips, in a circular, grinding motion, had Greg going nuts, trying to sit still.

Greg pulled his clean shaven cock out of his zipper and slowly began to stroke its swollen head. He stroked evenly and gently, taking care to pull the fold of skin up over the rim each and every time he jerked out a stroke. His masculine hands looked so damn good, jacking his cock, thought Starr. He was actually getting her pussy wetter than fuck. She could feel the seam of her hot, little shorts, wiggling between her pussy lips and that made her moist and horny. She sat down in a chair, in front of him and straddled her legs out to the sides, as far as she could, fucking, get them. She was humping that chair with all her might, trying not to let Greg know that she, herself, was trying to have a hot orgasm. She could squirm around sexily and still be able to scrape that pointed clit hood against the cushion and make it stand straight up. Starr had massive pussy lips and a clit. Her pink lips were well known for falling out of one side of her shorts, or both, and causing instant boners.

If her lips, or at least one of them, did this, Starr would always seductively reach down and either look surprised that she was exposed and try to stuff the lip back in, or she'd inadvertently pull it out more and wince. She had been known to drive cocks absolutely wild with her routine of pulling her pussy lips off to an orgasm. All the while, she was sitting there talking, but squirting at the same time, and ever so lightly squirming in her chair. She could talk about the stocks and have a massive orgasm, by nonchalantly fingering those lips.

Starr had always been very sexual. Ever since she could remember having a pussy, she had been masturbating it, once or twice, each and every day. Many times, she took a public restroom break opportunity and jacked off in their stall, with girls on either side of her. She knew there were times she was infectious and caused fellow women to become as horny and amorous as her. She could smell the strong scent of pussy and even hear herslick pussy, as fingers took the nasty plunge. Women had a unique way of sniffing out pussy, at the drop of the hat.

Starr could get around a girl and smell her pussy cum. It got her hot, most of the time.

As of lately, Starr was not afraid to admit that she and her best friend, Robin, had been fucking and wanting one another. They only started the month before. They had gotten wet for one another for years, but never gave in to the temptation.

One day, Robin and Starr were just too hot to hold back. Starr was trying on super short shorts and her, damn, lips kept protruding out of her tiny shorts. Robin couldn't help but stare at those fucking, hot lips of Starr's – especially, when she yanked them out real far and pulled them hard. She has also seen Starr flick the hood of her clit so hard it turned red as fire. She flicked and flicked, until wads of white cream poured out and made seductive cum strands from Starr's middle finger. She'd torture that damn clit until it got so big it looked like a little dick. She'd take the very tip of her finger and flick so lightly you could see the clit jump. Even though Starr was a very kindhearted woman, she was also nasty and sexy as hell.

Starr was considering all of these sexual delights, as she watched Greg stroke his muscle to a hot orgasm, about the exact, same, time her squirting orgasm started. It was ultra-erotic how they sat, face to face, in chairs, getting off, unable to touch each other. The phenomenon of forbidden love and lust has always driven human beings wild, sexually. It was still intact, as a phenomenon, with Starr and Greg, and was taking place right at that moment.

Greg's private dance time was over and he and Starr just looked at each other, not knowing exactly what to say next. Suddenly, Greg spoke up, "Would you like to go out to dinner some evening with me?" he asked.

"I'm off on Sunday," replied Starr.

"Okay, how about I pick you up at 7?" asked Greg.

"Sure!" said Starr, and she jotted down her address and phone number for Greg, on a piece of paper.

Monday rolled around and Starr was anxious about her date with Greg. It had been several months since Starr had been out with a man. She didn't have such a good track record with them. Right out of high school, Starr had gotten involved in a relationship, and all that did was lead to abuse. Now, at 25, Starr was bound, and determined, to never be the victim of an abusive man, again.

At seven O'clock, on the nose, Greg rang Starr's doorbell. She was very excited to see him. She opened the door and Greg's chin about dropped to the ground. Starr looks absolutely breathtaking. She had her beautiful long, blonde hair curled in sexy waves and a tight black, cocktail dress, with a mini skirt and high heel strappy, black shoes. "You look amazing," said Greg to

Starr, practically drooling.

"Thank you. You don't look so bad yourself," said Starr.

They walked outside and Greg opened the door for Starr, letting her inside his BMW. "This is sure a sweet ride," said Starr.

"Thank you," said Greg. "Do you like seafood?" asked Greg.

"Sure, I love it," replied Starr.

"We are going to a place where we can eat outside, on the deck, and see the stars in the sky," said Greg.

When they arrived at the restaurant, Greg went to Starr's side of the BMW and took her hand, to help her out of the car. They shared a lovely dinner. Greg had the swordfish and steak platter, while Starr had the boiled shrimp and rice pilaf. The two of them talked and enjoyed each other's company, immensely. It seemed that they had a lot in common, and, of course, they were extremely attracted to one another.

Greg couldn't help his reactions. It seemed as if every time he got around Starr, for any length of time, he got a raging boner in his pants. It seemed she simply just had that effect on him. Little did Greg know Starr was thinking precisely the same thing about him and his very hot self. His all American good boy looks were always what had appealed to Starr, in the men that she dated.

"Would you like to go to my place, or your place, for a night cap?" asked Greg. "My place is just a few miles from here."

"Then, your place it is," said Starr.

They got to Greg's house and he turned on some light music, and got them both a glass of red wine. They sat down, on the sofa, and talked, as if they had known each other for years.

"What made you want to become a stripper, Starr?" asked Greg, who truly was curious.

"I think I started for the wrong reasons, you know, for male attention, but then, I found out that it really is a lot of hard work. Plus, I enjoy dressing up and trying to look beautiful," said Starr.

"You do look beautiful, indeed. In fact, I have a feeling you would look beautiful in an old rag," said Greg, peering sexily into Starr's pale blue eyes. Greg started to stroke her lovely blonde hair. It felt like spun silk on his fingers. Starr closed her eyes. She absolutely loved her hair touched and stroked. She let out a sultry moan that drove Greg wild with wanting and need.

Greg reached in, toward Starr's beautiful red lips, and started to kiss her, passionately. Starr returned the kiss with red hot fervency. Greg was lighting a burning desire within her, and she wanted him to fuck her.

"Fuck me, Greg!" said Starr, in a horny tone of voice.

"I am going to fuck you, alright! I am going to fuck you seven ways to Sunday!"

The two of them kissed each other ravenously and made their way into Greg's room, where he fucked her hard, against the wall. She took his dick inside of her, hard, fast, and deep. They didn't even bother to remove their clothes. They were so hungry for each other. He lifted Starr's dress up, to reveal her hairless snatch, and was pleased to see she wasn't wearing any panties. She pulled his stiff rod out, from his zipper, and he plunged his steel meat in her like there was no tomorrow.

Greg's cock was perfect, thought Starr. It was 8 inches of thick girth and bulging head that felt good, as it bumped its way inside of her hungry and slippery pussy. Starr, then, got on the bed, in the doggie-style position, and poked her pussy out there for Greg to see.

"Damn, baby! That pussy looks inviting," said Greg. Just then, he plunged in deep, again. Greg loved looking at her long lips engulf his dick, as he fucked her brains out. "You have the sweetest pussy I have ever fucked, Starr," said Greg, as he decided to start fucking her slower and hotter.

He decided to tantalize her tight pussy a bit. So, Greg slowed the pace way down and very easily pulled his dick in and out of Starr's snatch, slow and measured. She could feel every single one of Greg's eight inches, as he slowly pulled it in and out of her. Starr especially loved it when she felt his rim pop inside of her. He had a bulging head on his cock that made her pussy wet with white cream. The slower he screwed Starr, the closer she was getting to an eruption of orgasmic juices.

Greg couldn't take it any longer. He needed to shoot his cock off, big time. He picked up the pace, again, and fucked Starr harder than he had ever fucked a woman before. She could feel his cum packed balls slapping her tight ass, as he yanked his cock in and out of her.

Just then, Greg's dick got hard as a rock and stiff as steel. He let out a loud moan and Starr could feel, inside her steaming pussy, that Greg was shooting his wads, and it made Starr spill her pussy juice all over his cock in reciprocation. Together, the two of them came in harmony that helped them reach peaks of ecstasy that were unbelievable.

After a few hours of simply basking in the afterglow of their lovemaking, Greg offered to take Starr home, if she wanted. Starr loved the idea that he gave her a choice. Greg treated Starr like a human and she wasn't accustomed to that, at all. Starr was used to men treating her like a piece of ass or a piece of meat. Greg seemed different. He was considerate and kind.

Starr could truly see herself falling for this guy, if she didn't watch out. She had been considering becoming a lesbian, because of the way she had been treated, by men, but Greg was changing all of that in a very good way. Starr got up and put her dress back on. Then, Greg drove her home. Like the gentleman that he was, he saw her to the door and gave her a long, passionate, kiss in her doorway. Starr fell into a peaceful sleep that night, with Greg on her mind, and quickly becoming a regular visitor in her heart.

The next morning, Starr woke up rested and happy. She took her shower and got ready to do her workout routine. Robin showed up at her usual time. She could tell that something was on Starr's mind, because Starr was unusually quiet. Finally, Robin went up to Starr and tried to French kiss her, but Starr kind of turned away.

"What's wrong, sweetheart?" asked Robin.

"Nothing really, I just don't want you to be too upset with me," replied Starr.

"Why would I be upset with you?" asked Robin. Starr then filled Robin in on Greg and told her how she thought she was beginning to have feelings for him.

Robin embraced Starr and explained to her that she would never be upset with her about that, and she understood. Starr was so pleased and was instantly reminded of why she thought Robin was such a terrific best friend.

A few hours later, Starr was getting prepared for her show at the club, that evening, and Greg stopped by to see her and chit chat.

Before either of them knew it, the chit chat turned to Greg's head between Starr's legs, eating the fuck out of her bald pussy. "You taste just as sweet as sugar, Starr. This is the best pussy I have ever eaten bar none," said Greg, as he came up for air.

Starr playfully pushed Greg's head back down, between her legs, and arched her pussy up, toward him, as if to say eat me! Starr absolutely loved the way Greg's hot mouth felt on her pussy and the way his mustache tickled her clit while he ate her out. Starr started to feel the beginnings of an orgasm.

Then, she asked Greg to fuck her. He excitedly rose up and laid her down. He plunged his dick deep inside her. He kissed her, so that she could taste her horny pussy all over his face and mustache. A couple of good tastes and Starr was shooting her pussy all over Greg's hot rod. Starr's orgasm made Greg spew his seed deep inside Starr's slick pussy.

After they got cleaned up from their afternoon sex fest, Starr and Greg spent a bit of time talking and getting to know one another a little more. Greg explained to Starr that he might not make it to her performance that night because a case he was working on required him to work over time that night. He told her he might be able to swing by, after the show, if that was alright for her. She told him it would be fine.

Starr performed her show three times and was really beginning to feel the burn in her muscles. Her show wasn't just some striptease act. She did a real workout routine and her gorgeous body showed it. Starr was actually thinking about going in the dressing room for a break, when she had a sudden request for a private dance.

Starr smiled, thinking it was probably Greg trying to surprise her, so she accepted the request.

When Starr went back, to the private dance area/room, she was surprised to see a total stranger sitting there. She totally believed that the man who had requested the private dance was Greg, especially when it was getting so late and close to time for the Silver Chalice to shut down for the night. In fact, several of the dancers had already gone home for the evening.

Starr thought, just do the dance Starr, then, maybe, Greg will show up and take you home and make love to you. Starr started to perform a bit, for the stranger, who frankly had an odd and disturbing look on his face. Starr just continued to do her dance, knowing that it would soon be over. She tried her best not to look in the freak's face too close. She could see he was getting aroused by the bulge in his pants and also by the fact that he was starting to rub the disgusting bulge.

Starr was thinking about backing out of this gig, when suddenly, the guy stood up and grabbed for her tit. Starr kind of pushed him away and told him that he wasn't allowed to touch her. She remembered how the two burly bouncers had just left for the evening. Starr was starting to get scared. There were a few people still around, but she doubted they would hear her, if she were to scream. She tried to fight the stranger, but he became increasingly more violent.

He grabbed her and put his hand over her mouth and said, "Make another sound, cunt, and I will slit your throat."

Starr shook her head, yes, and tears started to well up in her eyes.

The stranger slapped her hard across the face and ripped her top open, exposing her breasts. He grabbed one and started sucking it vehemently and biting her. Starr had a knee jerk reaction and punched him as hard as she could in the face, and then she tried to run. He grabbed her by her leg. Then, he hit her real hard, in the face, busting her nose. Blood came pouring out of Starr's nose, profusely.

She still tried to fight the evil monster, though. But, he grabbed a hold of her and ripped her pants down. He rammed his fingers inside her pussy, hurting Starr bad enough it made her wince in pain.

The rapist was pulling his pants down and exposing his disgusting cock and said, "I am going to fuck you, whore!"

Just around that time, a voice from behind the creep said, "Over my dead body, you son of a bitch."

It was Greg! He had told Starr he might come by after her show and he apparently meant it. Greg grabbed the bastard and started beating the shit out of him. He yelled for Starr to call the police and 911, as he threw her his cell phone. Starr was visibly shaken, but she managed to make the call. Soon, thereafter, the police and paramedics arrived.

Greg spent that time comforting Starr

and hugging her close. She was understandably shook up.

"Thank you for coming to my rescue. I don't know what I would have done, if not for you," said Starr.

"You do not have to say anything, beautiful, I am just glad that creep didn't hurt you any worse than he did," said Greg.

The paramedics checked Starr out, thoroughly, and bandaged her up.

Greg offered to drive Starr home and stay with her that night. Once they got to Starr's house, Greg pampered her and drew a nice warm bubble bath. He washed her hair and rinsed it for her and then helped her get into bed.

"Will you lay by me, tonight?" asked Starr.

"Of course, I will," said Greg. Greg held Starr, all night long, and didn't let her go once. He and Starr both knew that something incredible was happening between them. Starr knew, deep down in her heart, that Greg was the man of her dreams and her knight in shining armor. She had plans to marry this man, one day. He would find out soon enough, thought Starr, as she smiled and drifted off to sleep in Greg's arms.

2 SECOND CHANCES

(6 months ago)

Aubrey hurriedly put her things into her book bag. She desperately needed to get to the library before it closed. Her internet had gone down that day and she had to answer her email and check out a few other things on the web. She would also use any excuse to get away from Barry, her husband of 11 years. He was a narcissist, to put it lightly. There was no love left between them, but Aubrey was too afraid to leave him and get out on her own. Barry was emotionally, and at times physically, abusive to Aubrey. He did drugs, ran around on her and, all in all, was a terrible husband.

Aubrey was a sad and lost 45-year-old woman. She had no friends and was desperately in need of attention of any kind.

The library was a place she liked to go where she could feel at home and in her element. She loved browsing the books and using the internet. She could look at anything she wanted to, without Barry breathing down her neck. Aubrey headed out to her car and drove to the library. Barry was working late tonight so she could stay if she needed to. She drove into the library, parked her car and went inside.

She scanned the computer area and saw there were only three other people there; a girl, who was about eleven, an older woman, and a man, who was about fifty.

Aubrey made her way over to her favorite computer that was across from the man. She started to read her email and do a few searches of different things that interested her. She looked up a few times to see the man looking at her from time to time. Aubrey had to admit he was quite handsome and had a great smile. Aubrey flashed him the best smile she had. For some reason she was enjoying this little bit of attention.

She began to get enthralled by what she was reading and didn't even notice the handsome stranger sauntering her way until, suddenly, she heard a voice to her right.

"Excuse me. Do you happen to have a pencil? It seems someone took all the ones from my computer desk," the man asked.

Aubrey looked into the little basket sitting by the computer and said, "Yes, here you go," and offered him a choice of little mini pencils from the basket.

"Thank you very much. I cannot help but notice that you are looking up Mark Twain, I love him! I have his entire collection at home," the stranger told her.

As he was speaking, Aubrey noticed that he was incredibly handsome and even more so up close. He had rugged good looks with a hint of class that intrigued her. His eyes were a chocolate brown that were rich and vibrant; his hair was a stunning salt and pepper gray, and he had a full beard that really turned her on. She had always wondered what it felt like to kiss a man with a beard. He was a bit heavy set for her liking, but she found it kind of charming in a snugly sort of way.

The man took notice of Aubrey as well. She looked like a woman that had been through a lot but she had a sexy essence about her that was such a turn on. Her hair was a deep brown, about shoulder length and straight. She had steel blue eyes and beautiful fair skin. She was also a very petite woman, weighing about one hundred and five pounds at the most. He loved petite women.

"Would you like to have a cup of coffee with me in the café?" He asked her. "We could discuss Mark Twain at length."

Aubrey really wanted to but she wondered if she should, then before thinking she blurted out, "Okay. By the way my name is Aubrey what's yours?"

"Pardon me for not saying. My name is Tim and it's very nice to meet you Aubrey."

"Nice to meet you as well," the two of them shook hands and Aubrey felt a tingle run through her body. There was something truly wonderful about Tim but she wasn't quite sure what it was yet.

The two of them talked over two cups of

coffee and their conversation was so relaxed and easy, as if they had known each other forever.

"Oh my goodness, the time!" exclaimed Aubrey as she looked at her watch. "I have to be going now," she told him.

"Already?" sked Tim, "How about we meet up here tomorrow and maybe go for a walk? Or go for lunch?"

Before considering her reply, Aubrey found herself agreeing again to his request. "What time would you like to meet?" she asked.

"How about around eleven am?" suggested Tim.

"Okay, eleven it is," replied Aubrey, "see you then." Aubrey rushed out the door and headed home, hoping that Barry wasn't already there waiting for her.

Much to her dismay, Barry's van was in the driveway. Shit, thought Aubrey. She walked into the house and Barry greeted her with a string of accusatory questions.

"Where in the fuck were you? I was worried," said Barry.

"I'm fine, Barry, it's no big deal. I just lost track of time at the library looking up some stuff about authors and books," replied Aubrey. "I'm tired so I'm going to bed."

She was in no mood for Barry's controlling shit tonight. All she could think about was Tim. He was on her mind for some reason and she got the feeling that's where he was going to stay for a while.

The next morning Aubrey got up early. She had her lunch date and nothing else on her mind. She figured the earlier she got up and got rid of Barry the better. She hated to feel this way, but she could not stand the man she was married to. He had lied to her and cheated on her so many times, he had killed the love between them. Aubrey used to adore him, but not anymore. All she felt was disgust when she looked at him.

Once Barry went off to work, Aubrey began to get ready for her date with Tim. She knew she should feel guilty about having lunch with another man but she didn't. In her eyes, Barry deserved it. He was a pig and she didn't care whether he got hurt.

Aubrey showered and styled her hair in a chic pony tail and she put on just a touch of makeup and pretty pink lip gloss. Aubrey wasn't quite sure what to wear but finally decided upon a pink silk blouse and a cream colored slinky skirt. She looked sexy without coming off too slutty. She put on a pair of strappy cream colored sandals to finish off her look. She took one last glance in the mirror and at about 10:40 am, she headed for the library to meet Tim.

When Aubrey pulled into the library parking lot she saw Tim immediately. He did a friendly wave and gestured for her to park beside him. Aubrey pulled into the spot right beside Tim and he came over to her door to greet her.

"Hi beautiful, how are you today?" asked Tim.

"I'm doing very well, how about you?" Aubrey replied, blushing just a little.

"I'm doing perfectly. So do you want to take my car and go grab a bite to eat now?" asked Tim.

"Sure," said Aubrey, "I'm game for whatever you have planned."

Tim opened up the passenger's side for Aubrey and she climbed inside. Tim noticed that she had beautiful legs that were almost athletic in appearance. He also noticed that she was revealing a bit of cleavage and that she had nice firm breasts.

Aubrey sensed that Tim liked what he saw and she smiled up at him seductively. She was definitely starved of attention and Tim's was just what the doctor ordered.

As they drove towards the café, where they planned to eat lunch, there was a sexual tension in the air that could not be denied. It was so heavy that it was very uncomfortable.

Aubrey would sneak a glance at Tim's strong hands as he clutched the steering wheel. Tim would sneak a peek at Aubrey's thighs as she switched positions, indicating she was uncomfortable but turned the fuck on.

Tim felt the beginnings of a hard on in his jeans. He wondered if Aubrey noticed. This woman was making him aroused and there was nothing he could do to stop his cock from growing. Tim could sear the smell of her was in the air. Aubrey opened her thighs just enough for Tim to see she had no panties on. He let out an audible groan that could not be ignored.

"You know what? My house is close to here. Would you like to see it? You could see my Mark Twain collection."

"Okay," Aubrey said eagerly. They both knew that what they wanted to see had nothing to do with Samuel Clements.

Tim pulled into his carport with a screeching halt and practically leapt from his seat. His cock was extremely hard right now and very uncomfortable indeed.

Aubrey followed, just as eager. As they got to the door Tim turned the key. Almost before he got the door shut behind him, they attacked each other like two wild animals. The attraction was intense.

Tim ravaged Aubrey's hot body right there, by the front door. She lifted her leg up over his hips just begging for that boner inside of her hungry, wet snatch. Tim looked down and saw her pussy wide open and starving, just begging to be fucked – hard!

Aubrey unzipped his pants and his cock popped out like a jack in the box. She was so hungry for him she didn't hesitate to arch her wet pussy towards his cock, begging him to enter her. Tim plunged inside Aubrey so deep she winced with lust and pleasure like an animal. He literally ripped her pink silk blouse off, revealing her peach colored swollen nipples that almost spoke to him to suck the fuck out of them. Tim was so ravenous he literally sucked both salacious breasts at the same time. The concupiscence in the room hung like a seductive cloud over their heads urging them on towards the throes of raw passion.

"My God, you taste delicious," said Tim, as he ravaged her neck, throat and chest.

"You are making me so hot I may come all over the floor if you don't take me to your bed soon," said a horny Aubrey. "Oh Tim, Fuck me now!" she begged. "I mean fuck me hard and deep."

Tim carried this very passionate and yearning woman to his bed and did just that over and over again. He banged her hard and fast until his balls made a slapping sound that echoed off the walls. It made Tim almost explode inside her luscious, thrashing body, but he wanted her to mount him reverse cowgirl style and give it to him hard.

"Fuck me cowgirl style and do it now baby!" begged Tim.

Aubrey flipped to the top of his body and first faced him with her perfect tits swinging right in front of his hungry eyes. The look in her eyes was of raw, unadulterated desire. Then without his bulging dick ever budging, she turned around and rode him in reverse. He could see her dark hair tossing in front of him and watched his cock being gripped by her long lips as it moved in and out of her hard and fast. Aubrey ground and bounced on top of his cock so hard that her pussy wasn't letting go until it was filled with a hot load his spunk. They came the moment her pussy grasped his cock in a last futile effort to squeeze it dry. They collapsed in an orgasmic haze that left them breathless and panting, knowing full well that was the best fucking sex either of them had ever had.

"Wow," said Tim as soon as he regained his breath.

"I know, right?" said Aubrey. "That was incredible!"

"I think it is fair to say that we have a connection of some kind," said Tim.

"You think?" asked Aubrey, kind of giggling. They both embraced and laughed for about ten solid minutes, rolling around on Tim's bed butt naked.

"So since I didn't buy you lunch how about I make you lunch?" Tim asked.

"It sounds nice, but don't feel obligated." replied Aubrey.

"My pleasure, now come with me to the kitchen." said Tim. The two of them laughed and talked about all kinds of things that interested them. Aubrey couldn't believe that she had actually met a man that liked books and talking about them.

They ate ham sandwiches, potato chips and dill pickles with a bottle of white wine.

"Tim I need to tell you something." Tim put his index finger to her lips to quiet her.

"I know, you're married, right?" said Tim.

"How did you know?" asked Aubrey.

"It was fairly obvious from the moment I met you, that's all," said Tim. Aubrey didn't know why but she felt so relaxed with Tim, and she opened up and told him all the details of her marriage.

Tim felt so fucking bad for Aubrey. She was a wonderful and amazing woman. It was plain to see. How could this prick Barry treat her like this? Was he fucking nuts?

"Aubrey, I am sorry you are treated this way and stuck in a loveless marriage, but maybe I can help you." said Tim.

"How so?" asked Aubrey.

"Well, for starters I can invite you out to my deck to enjoy a relaxing hot tub experience. How about a little afternoon delight?"

"It sounds absolutely delightful and very relaxing." The two of them headed out to the deck into the pleasantly warm South California air. California in June was a beautiful place to be and the weather was near perfect. Aubrey just realized that she didn't have her swimsuit.

"What am I going to wear in here?" She asked.

"Your birthday suit is fine by me," giggled Tim. Aubrey took her towel and began to pop Tim with it in a playful manner until he pretend tackled her right into a chaise recliner out on the deck. She landed on top of him and couldn't help but notice that Tim's cock was hard again. They started to French kiss quite vehemently; their bodies pressing close together, yearning for hotter sex and steamy romance.

"Let's get in the hot tub," said Tim, "maybe we can come close to rubbing one out and then fuck out here on the deck." So they got in the tub and Tim watched as Aubrey's nipples became rock hard. It made him start slowly stroking his dick under water. He'd yank it just enough to let the head peek up above the water looking with one eye at Aubrey longingly. Tim could tell Aubrey was toying with her fuzzy pussy underwater. It fucking turned him on to think so and he tried his hardest to hear her slippery snatch underneath that fuzzy muff.

They looked at each other with wanton eyes as they mutually jacked their way to near orgasm. Tim motioned to Aubrey to stand up and follow him out of the hot tub. Once outside of the tub they went at it like a couple of sex starved nymphomaniacs. Tim laid Aubrey down on the chaise lounge and ravaged her pussy with his face and tongue.

"Fuck, you taste like candy. This is a delicious pussy you got, sugar!" said Tim who was tossing his head back and forth in a sideways motion, eating Aubrey out like nobody's business.

"Your beard feels so good tickling the head of my clit," said Aubrey, "I think I might cum if you keep that up." Tim broke into an all-out, muff diving fest that led Aubrey to nearly scream, she fought to contain it because they were outdoors. After coming, she said to him,

"Straddle my face baby and I'll swallow your balls deep."

"Mmm, that sounds fucking wonderful," said Tim. He straddled Aubrey and shot wads of hot cream straight down her throat. After the partaking of their afternoon delights together, Aubrey and Tim talked about their hopes, their dreams, and their plans for the future.

"Did you not want kids with Barry?" asked Tim.

"No, not really, Barry is too volatile. I wouldn't want to bring a kid up around him and his temper," said Aubrey. "Also I can't have kids. At least that's what the doctor told me," replied Aubrey.

"I'd better get going Tim!" exclaimed Aubrey. "If I'm not home in time to cook his dinner, he gets irate."

"Okay doll, I'll drive you back to the library to get your car." When they arrived at the library parking lot, Aubrey and Tim exchanged a long, lingering, wet kiss. "I gave you my cell number. Call me," said Tim.

"I will darling," said Aubrey. They both knew that they were already falling deeply in love. It was a cosmic connection that was impossible to miss.

At home that evening Aubrey was fucking miserable. Now that she had the taste of pleasure and attraction, Barry seemed more unbearable than ever. She snuck off to the bathroom to get herself a 'Tim fix'. Tim answered in his velvety voice,

"Heyyyy baby!" Aubrey smiled from ear to ear.

"Hi handsome, what's going on?" asked Aubrey.

"Your lingering scent is hanging in the air." said Tim sexily.

"God I miss you," said Aubrey. "Living with this moron is getting worse by the second. Since I have dipped my hot pink toes in the river of Tim, I never want to return to the murky waters called Barry." said Aubrey.

Tim started talking very erotically and got her all hot and bothered. She was hoping Barry would hit the sack early so she might have a bit of big girl fun with her big girl toys.

When Aubrey went back to the living room, Barry had already turned in for the night. She could hear him snoring in the bedroom at the back of their house. She felt horny as hell and needed to relieve her agony soon. Thoughts of Tim's rigid cock got her all wet down stairs. She could feel the familiar twinges inside her pelvic region that told her she was about to be hot as fuck. Damn, she loved that feeling inside her. That warm and yummy feeling a woman gets when she's turned on.

That familiar almost cramp like feeling, without the pain, that hit the uterus sending horny waves of sex all over a girl's body. The tingling of her lips as they bulged and got bigger with every nasty thought. The urge to tickle her clit with the tips of her middle or index fingers became impossible to resist. The urge to tickle it ever so slightly right on the head sending pulses of erotic heat throughout every fold. Aubrey reached her fingers underneath her T-shirt to discover a drenched pussy that wanted one-on-one attention. The thought of getting caught just heightened her horny mood.

At first she liked to tease her tingling clit hood. She would flick it with the very tips of her fingers and stop. She would wait until her body responded with a jerking motion. Then Aubrey would administer a couple more flicks to the clit. Then she'd pull her lips real slow, just like when a man ate her lips out. She would make a sexy moan that made her horny as fuck. Her left lip was so sensitive she could hardly touch it without squirting her wads. She would quicken her flicking pace; she loved to watch her clit in a mirror. It produced white cream that would suddenly start oozing from her hot cunt. She would then take the pussy cream and smear it on one rock hard nipple and flick the nipple tip with her tongue and then ravenously suck it. She loved tasting her pussy on her tits.

Masturbation was something that Aubrey had always loved since she was fourteen. She remembers the night when she discovered her clit and clit hood. She remembers creaming all over her fingers for the first time. By this time, Aubrey was flicking the fuck out of her horny clit and yanking her lips vehemently. She was watching the pussy throb and getting so horny she nearly screamed. She knew in moments she would be humping her whole hand, trying to fist herself. She rode her hand hard. Grinding on it and churning her hips in a naughty motion that always got her coming like mad.

"Fuck!" growled Aubrey, "I'm about to squirt my nasty cunt!" And she did just that all over the sofa.

She reached over to click send on her computer. She had just videotaped her ultra-hot masturbation session for Tim as a surprise, boy would he ever be! At least she didn't get her cum all over her computer.

The days and weeks to come would be some of the best Aubrey and Tim had ever experienced. They couldn't stay apart for long. Aubrey was finding it more and more difficult to make up excuses to Barry as to why she was going to be home late, or why she didn't have supper on the table at precisely 6 o'clock.

She felt nervous about telling Barry that she had plans to go see a local play acting group that night at the library. Of course there was no play being performed, but Aubrey and Tim had very special plans that evening. She had a thing for lighthouses, so Tim had promised he'd take her to an old, abandoned lighthouse that hardly anyone else knew about, and that they would make love inside of it.

Of course there were rumors that some of the southern California lighthouses were haunted, but to Aubrey that just made the adventure all the more enchanting. After handing Barry an excuse and getting his dinner ready for him, Aubrey managed to sneak a few extra belongings in her bag and head out the door straight to Tim's place. She was so excited she could hardly contain herself. She had never been up close and personal with a lighthouse before and especially not in the arms of the man she loved and adored.

Once she arrived at Tim's it was already close to 6 o'clock.

"We better get going, beautiful," said Tim as they jumped into his Chevy and headed towards their destination. They held hands all the way, excited to extinguish (even if just a little bit) the burning desire within them. Once they arrived at the lighthouse location Aubrey and Tim got out into the breezy night air. They walked up and down the shore talking and laughing like two teenagers in love.

"Do you want to see the inside of the lighthouse?" asked Tim.

"Sure, catch me if you can!" said Aubrey and she took off running trying to entice Tim to chase her. They opened the creaky door to the lighthouse and Tim turned on the flashlight that he brought, along with other items packed for their romantic adventure.

"What else do you have in that bag?" asked Aubrey. Tim opened the bag revealing that it was full of interesting things. "Very nice, candles and blankets and wine!" said Aubrey.

"It's all for you, my love," said Tim.

Aubrey and Tim explored the intriguing lighthouse for a while until they decided to rest their legs a bit.

"I am chilly," said Aubrey.

"Come lie down with me on the blanket and I will warm you up," said Tim. He started to caress the soft and luscious folds of Aubrey's body watching her tremble with wanton desire. He desired to show Aubrey that he was her man and would be for as long as she'd have him. Tim licked his way down Aubrey's very curvaceous body until he reached her beautiful flower that was beginning to unfold before his very eyes. He lingered upon every succulent inch of her body, leaving no portion untouched or un-kissed.

"I want to taste your delicious flower, my love," Tim said as he went down between her milky thighs.

"You know exactly how to eat my pussy baby. It feels so good when you suck my lips" replied Aubrey. Tim licked her clit head to a throbbing hard on and then slowly but surely licked each lip until they were as long and red hot as he could get them.

Just when Aubrey thought she couldn't hold back her juices any longer, she squirmed and thrashed into an orgasmic state that blew her away. Tim had to try hard to keep her body still enough to suck every drop of her luscious nectar.

"That was amazing," said Aubrey. "I love you, Tim."

"I love you too, Aubrey, very much so," replied Tim. As he sat up from indulging in the pussy of his dreams, it was obvious he had just been eating pussy. His beard was wet with Aubrey's cum. He lay down beside her and they French kissed until every drop of her nectar was savored between them.

Suddenly Aubrey sat up and said, "Oh my God look at the time. I have to be getting back, Tim!"

"Okay, baby we'll go, don't worry." said Tim. He wished so much that Aubrey was his and that he didn't always have to return her to that creep Barry. Quickly, the two packed their belongings and headed down the coast towards San Diego.

Little did Aubrey know that while she was away at the lighthouse with Tim, Barry had done a bit of investigating as to where Aubrey was that evening. When she arrived home a very angry Barry met her at the door, "Where the fuck have you been? You slut," asked Barry in an angry and vicious tone.

"I told you I was going to see a play at the library. It went over some!" screamed Aubrey.

"Don't bullshit, me you fucking cunt!" screamed Barry and he slapped Aubrey's face, hard. Aubrey began to cry and scream at Barry to calm down. He slapped her hard again and pushed her into the end table.

"Calm down Barry. I can explain," cried Aubrey.

"You are a fucking whore and a nasty cunt. I can smell the screw you just had all over you!" Yelled Barry and he slapped Aubrey again. He took his hands and out and wrapped them around Aubrey's throat and said,

"You fucking bitch, if you ever fuck around on me again, I'll kill you and your lover Tim!"

Aubrey was shocked when Barry said Tim's name. "Go take a shower, you nasty whore, and wash his cock off of you." Aubrey stayed in the shower for 30 minutes letting the warm water rush over her body. She wept tears of pain, remorse and sadness. She knew what she had to do the next day.

Aubrey woke up the next morning sore and bruised from the night before. She felt sick to her stomach. Thank God Barry was gone. He always went in early on Fridays. Aubrey cried tears of sadness and picked up the phone.

"Hi baby," Tim said as he picked up the phone. "How's my best girl?

"Tim I need to tell you something. I've decided that we need to break this affair off," said Aubrey.

"What? Aubrey what are you saying? I love you," cried Tim.

"I don't love you, Tim. I was only using you for sex," said Aubrey.

"Aubrey, you don't mean that!" Aubrey hung up the phone before he could say another word and then went to her bedroom and cried into her pillow, feeling hopeless.

(2 months later)

Aubrey had been getting very sick and had finally made an appointment to see the doctor. It never dawned on her what it was. She had been told she couldn't have children, but the results from the pregnancy test were positive.

Aubrey was devastated. She felt trapped by Barry and was scared to death to leave him. She had no doubts that Barry would try to kill her if she did. But if he found out she was carrying a baby he would know for sure it wasn't his. She hadn't slept with Barry in nearly a year.

The baby was Tim's. That was a fact. How could she keep a fact like this from her baby's daddy? She couldn't. She had to tell Tim today. She was still crazy in love with Tim but she had no idea if he felt the same way. He had tried to reach her, but she ignored him any way that she could.

Tim had been depressed as hell since Aubrey broke his heart. He was still having trouble coming to terms with the break up. It had torn him apart. He knew he had to get back out there, but he simply wasn't ready.

Tim had prepared a sandwich and was just about to sit down and watch a movie when he heard the doorbell ring. He was kind of pissed off at first because he really just wanted to veg out for a while. When he opened the door, Tim was shocked, "Aubrey, what are you doing here?"

"If it's a bad time I can come back later," said Aubrey.

"Don't be ridiculous," said Tim. "Come on inside."

Aubrey broke down in uncontrollable tears. "Aubrey what is it? Baby, please say what's wrong?" he pleaded.

Aubrey began to recount the whole story starting at the part when Barry figured their affair out. "That son of a bitch!" yelled Tim. "I will kill him for laying a hand on you."

"Tim, please, I need to tell you something." said Aubrey. "I have never stopped loving you for one second and I am pregnant with your baby!" said Aubrey through tears.

"Aubrey, are you serious?" said Tim. "Oh my God, a baby, that is wonderful!" said Tim, until he began to think about it.

"Tim, Barry says he will kill us both. I'm scared Tim. I don't know what to do."

Tim sold insurance online and wrote news commentaries and articles so it was no problem for him to pick up and leave.

"Aubrey, listen to me. We can go far away from here and start a new life. We can have a family. You told me you always wanted a baby," said Tim.

"Yes I do, but how will we hide? What about the fact I will still be married to Barry legally?" asked Aubrey.

"Baby, I don't know the details but we can do it. Our love can get us through anything." Tim replied. Aubrey looked at Tim with love and trust in her eyes and said,

"Okay baby let's do it!" Tim embraced the woman that he loved and then gently rubbed her tummy and said, "I love you Aubrey. It will be okay I promise you. Come on, we need to pack some things and get out of here!" said Tim.

They took off about an hour later to their new destination. Would they be able to hide from Barry and have a new life?

3 RILEY'S SECRET

Trouble at the Bank

Riley Madison was just getting in her candy apple red convertible that fateful Monday morning when she got a call on her Android. "Oh shit," said Riley, "what is it now? A girl can't even get a cup of coffee down before the phone is ringing!" Needless to say Riley was not a morning person.

Riley Madison was a headstrong woman who was used to going after what she wanted. Riley was 5 feet 7 inches of solid muscle. She worked out daily and ran at least 7 miles a week. She kept her hair a no nonsense platinum blonde in a pixie cut and she had steel blue eyes that could cut right through you if need be. She had a body to die for and legs that went on forever.

But none of that was important to Riley.

Her job was everything to Riley. She had never been married and didn't have any kids. Riley Madison was a special agent with the FBI, and she was no stranger to adventure and danger.

She had climbed her way up the ladder of success the honest way. She followed in her dad's footsteps. He had died when Riley was only 16 years old. He had been shot down by a drug dealer in a drug raid in New York's inner city. Riley remembered it well. As she stood sobbing at her dad's grave she promised him one thing. She would follow in his footsteps and fight the bad guys for him.

After Riley graduated high school, she fulfilled her promise to her late dad and joined the New York City police force, later training for the FBI. Although because of her beauty and sex appeal she put up with all kinds of harassment from her fellow agents, Riley was tough as nails and didn't let it get to her.

Riley worked her ass off and moved up in rank quickly. Riley Madison was known to be one of the FBI's toughest agents. She didn't take shit from anybody, especially low lives like the ones who killed her dad, her hero.

Riley pushed the talk button on her cell only to hear startling news. On the other end of the line was her partner and good friend Joe Barillo. "Riley you need to get over to the New York First National Bank quick. We have a bad situation on going on here... possibly the mob or terrorists!" Riley didn't hesitate for a second but gunned her Camaro full speed ahead to First National Bank.

When Riley arrived there was mass confusion. Sirens were blaring, people were screaming and cops were fucking everywhere. Riley rushed up to a group of New York beat cops and flashed her FBI badge.

"What the fuck is going on here?" said Riley to the cops.

"As far as we can tell a couple of mobsters have the bank tellers and the patrons held hostage in there. It's a fucking nightmare," said the cop. "We have negotiators trying to talk the men out but no such luck.

"The loser in there is saying something about how an employee owed the mob money and they were going to get it one way or the other. A teller tripped the alarm and now we have a hostage situation." said the cop.

Suddenly gunshots were fired from inside the bank. That's all it took. Riley grabbed her gun from her holster and before she even realized what she was doing she headed inside the bank. She could hear Joe, her partner, screaming "No, Riley stop don't do it you'll get shot!"

She was oblivious to Joe's request. Riley was going to stop this bullshit right now! When Riley entered the bank she immediately came face to mask with one of the robbers or killers or whatever in the fuck they were. "Put your hands up now!" Riley said as she pointed her gun at the loser.

Just then she saw another masked man running for the back door. Riley pulled the trigger on her gun and the next thing she recalled was getting very drowsy and dizzy. Riley had been chloroformed and was now a long way from New York City aboard a yacht headed for a remote island.

Riley had been dreaming for what seemed like days and boy did she have a headache that would kill a horse. Riley was trying her hardest to get her eyes opened but they didn't seem to want to. She felt so groggy and she couldn't remember where she was or who she was at that moment. She racked her brain trying to recall.

Then suddenly it started to come back to her. As it started to return to her mind, Riley got frightened and then she went into defense mode. The last thing she remembered was getting bashed in the head and then getting dizzy. "Those fucking sons of bitches! What did they do to me and why?" whispered Riley under her breath.

Then it all flooded her mind the phone call from Joe, the conversation with the cop and the stand-off at the bank. She remembered barreling inside to chaos. She remembered drawing her gun and then pitch black.

As Riley began to gather her wits, she started to get pissed. What had happened to her? Were those assholes in the bank to blame? She deiced she was getting out of wherever she was and then suddenly she realized she was on a fucking ship! She could hear the water and waves and feel the slight movement. She could smell the sea. She had to get out of this bed they had her handcuffed to.

Riley started to tamper with the cuff. Damn

it! She would not be chained up like an animal. She started rattling the cuff with all of her might and cursing.

"Well, well what have we here? It seems the cop is awake," said some burly looking Italian buffoon who looked like his name could easily be Guido.

"What you have here is one pissed bitch!" said Riley. "Take these fucking handcuffs off me now," Riley demanded.

The buffoon began to laugh so hard he almost quit breathing. Then he said "Hey Vinny did you hear the queen, she wants me to cut her loose!"

Riley could hear the roar of laughter coming from down a small hall.

"I want to speak to whoever's in charge!" demanded Riley.

She heard yet another roar of laughter and the goon actually has to sit down. "Calm down, hot stuff. We ain't gonna hurt ya or nothing ... although you are pretty foxy!" More laughs from the hall come Riley's direction.

"Hey! Watch your mouth, you low life! I'll kick your ass all over this boat."

"Oh, I am so scared," says the lowlife.

"Shut up and get me whoever is in charge of this fiasco right now!" Riley screamed.

Then suddenly another voice that Riley hadn't heard started to speak: "I am the boss around here ma'am, how can I help you this morning?" Riley looked up and saw the most handsome and sexy man she had ever fucking laid eyes on. Riley fainted dead on the spot.

When she finally came to again, Riley looked at him kind of perplexed and said,

"How can you help me?" She said it again. "How can you help me? Gee! I don't know. Maybe you could tell me why you kidnapped me?" Riley said in a very sarcastic and angry tone.

"Don't you think you need to calm down ma'am? You've had a long couple of days and you must be tired," said the stranger.

"No I don't need to calm down. I need to know who you are and why I am here," Riley exclaimed.

"Allow me to introduce myself. My name is Angelo Russo and I do believe yours is Riley Morgan... am I correct?"

"How did you know that?" asked Riley.

"I have my connections," said Angelo. Riley couldn't help but thinking that this man was so fucking hot and she could swear he was getting her wet.

Down girl, thought Riley, you can't let this incredibly sexy man get your pussy in a tantrum.

Angelo couldn't help but notice that he was getting to this woman he could almost smell her scent. She was "getting to" him as well. He felt a bulge in his slacks that he quickly tried to hide by moving "it" over a bit through his pocket.

Of course Riley was sharp and noticed this man must be getting a boner for her. So she ever so slightly showed him a little nipple by leaning forward just a bit and giving him a peek. That did it! Angelo was mysteriously turned on instantly by this gorgeous blonde he had captive on his yacht.

Angelo cleared his throat, adjusted his huge

Italian cock again and said, "Would you like to join me for lunch out on the deck?" Before she knew it, Riley was saying, "Yes, that would be great. And then maybe you can tell me why I'm here."

"You will find some clothes and linens in the closet over there," Angelo pointed across the cabin. "I'll lock the door and have the steward come and get you in 45 minutes. Now let me unlock your cuff."

Angelo bent over her to unlock her and he smelled so amazing and he was pure sex rolled into one handsome package. Riley knew at this moment she was wildly attracted to Angelo and that they would be together for a long time. Riley had great intuition. This will have to be your secret, she thought to herself.

The steward came and got Riley at 12 noon on the dot. She was showered and wearing a bright red cocktail dress that showed off her svelte body perfectly. She had her platinum blonde pixie hair slicked back in a very chic style. She had on a pair of black stilettos that always made her feel powerful. Just because she was a prisoner didn't mean she couldn't look sexy.

It was rather odd that these clothes fit her perfectly though. As Riley approached the table where Angelo sat his jaw nearly hit the floor. She looked gorgeous, thought Angelo. He couldn't help but be wildly attracted to her.

"Hi there Angelo," said Riley.

"Hello Ms. Morgan thank you for joining me," said Angelo as he got up to help her get seated.

"You can call me Riley. Why the hell not?" she said. As the first course was brought to them Riley began to question Angelo. "Okay tell me why did you kidnap me?" asked Riley.

"It's a long story Riley. I am a mob boss. Does that surprise you?" said Angelo. "And you happened to be in the wrong place at the wrong time. We mean you no harm, but yet I have no idea what to do with you," said Angelo.

"How about let me go home and we'll forget this even happened?" said Riley coyly.

"I cannot do that Riley. You are FBI. You will immediately have me arrested," replied Angelo.

"Yes you are probably right," said Riley. Angelo could not believe the balls of this woman. It turned him on completely.

"So why were you robbing the bank or whatever you guys were doing there?" asked Riley.

"I may as well just tell you," said Angelo wiping the corners of his mouth with the stark white napkin. "There was a worker at the bank who owed the family money. I was instructed by my father to get the money. So I did what my father asked of me. Well let's just say I tried to," said Angelo very nervously. Riley detected fear in Angelo's voice. "Would you care to dance?" Angelo asked Riley and held out his hand for her to take.

"Sure, why not?" replied Riley taking his

strong hand.

As their bodies swayed to the music they couldn't help but feel the sparks between them. It was an undeniable attraction that didn't look like it was going to subside. Angelo held Riley close as the fire heated up between them.

Before either of them could stop the progression they were kissing each other ravenously. Angelo kissed the front of Riley's neck down her throat sending shock waves through her body. Her pussy tingled and got drenched immediately. Riley kissed Angelo back with fervor making his penis grow to where it felt it might pop right out of his slacks. "Do you want to go to my room here on the yacht?" said Angelo in a seething growl.

"Fuck yes, I do," replied Riley in a sexy voice that drove Angelo wild.

They barely got the door shut in Angelo's cabin before they were ripping each other's clothes off. Angelo pulled Riley's long leg up to his waist and plunged his throbbing member (that was now standing straight out from his zipper) inside of her. He made love to her hard right up against the door. Each plunge of his massive dick made Riley wince and moan with pleasure. Without removing his cock he picked Riley up and she held on with both legs wrapped around his waist and he fucked her so hard they both exploded in orgasmic spasms that made them want each other all the more. Angelo took Riley to the bed lifted her short skirt and asked her.

"Can I eat your incredibly hot pussy?" asked Angelo.

"Not only can you eat it," said Riley, "I demand that you do."

"Mmmmm that's my girl," said Angelo as he buried his head in her hairy snatch. "I love hairy pussy," he murmured. "I haven't had one in a while. You taste absolutely delicious."

As Angelo went back down on her pussy with vehemence. Riley ground her pussy and hips into Angelo's face hard and fast.

"Fuck, you eat me good," said Riley. "I am going to squirt my juices all over your face." she said in a sexy growl.

Angelo moved his head from side to side burying his tongue deep inside Riley's pussy hole. "I am about to cummmmmm...." hollered Riley and she let out a scream that turned Angelo on big time. Riley released her nectar all over Angelo's face. Angelo groaned out very loudly and then went back up to Riley and let her kiss her cream from his mouth. He fucked her mouth hard with his tongue.

"Mmm, I taste good," said Riley as she ravenously ate her own juices from Angelo's soaked mouth. They both collapsed breathless and unkempt upon the mattress. "So... now what?" said Riley. Riley and Angelo knew that they were connected for a long time now.

Angelo and Riley drifted off to sleep. About three hours later, Riley woke up groggy as hell and found herself nuzzled up closer to her captor. She thought to herself, God, Riley, what is wrong with you... have you lost it? This man kidnapped you.

She then looked over at Angelo and thought how handsome and sexy he was. She also felt that underneath his rough exterior somehow lay a sensitive man; as crazy as it sounded even to her, Riley was almost certain she was right. Angelo groaned a sleepy groan and opened his eyes slowly to see the beautiful blonde lying in his arms. "Hi beautiful, what time is it?" said Angelo.

"Time for me to get back to my own cabin," said Riley as she began to get up.

"Don't go," said Angelo looking at Riley irresistibly. Just then he pulled Riley into him and kissed her passionately and sweetly. They kissed for several minutes very slowly and seductively. This man had a power over her that no man ever had thought Riley. Was she falling for a criminal?

After their long and passionate kiss, Angelo and Riley spent several hours talking and taking a bubble bath. Later, Angelo ordered dinner for them in his cabin which had a skylight with the stars beaming down. "You look stunning tonight, Riley," said Angelo.

Riley had no makeup on and just one of Angelo's shirts on but she felt more alive than she had in ages. "Thank you. Angelo can I ask you a question?" said Riley. "What did you mean earlier when you said you tried to fulfill your father's wishes?"

"Oh it is nothing for you to worry about, my dear. Now eat your lobster."

"Look, Angelo, I'm not some little kid you can boss around or one of your goons. I need to know exactly what I am involved with here."

"No, you don't Riley!" said Angelo in a tone that said he was about done talking. "Look Riley, I will find a way to keep you safe you just have to let me think about it okay?"

Riley decided just to be quiet about it for the time being and let Angelo do just what he said. Riley decided to walk out the French doors and go out onto the deck. A few moments later Angelo walked out with two glasses and a bottle of champagne. "Care for a glass of bubbly my lady?" asked Angelo in his most romantic tone.

Riley couldn't help but smile. "Okay thank you." She replied.

Riley and Angelo sat out on the deck for three hours and chatted and talked about everything under the sun. They had a real connection. They both desired to make their dads proud although for very different reasons.

As crazy as it sounded, Riley felt like she had known Angelo her whole life. She felt like they had a connection, sort of like star crossed lovers. Riley felt like she was falling for Angelo. She knew it was ludicrous and surely it was the champagne. Little did Riley know Angelo was feeling much the same way. Little did Riley know Angelo desired to make passionate love to her right then and right there and there wasn't anything she could do about it.

Riley was getting very tired and Angelo could tell. "How about we go inside?" suggested Angelo.

"Okay," said Riley. As they got inside Angelo grabbed Riley and planted another passionate kiss on her soft lips. This time, Riley was taken in by the warmth and magic between them. For some reason she had no desire to ever be apart from this man ever again. She didn't know why or how, but she was falling for Angelo. Was she insane? She was falling for a mobster, a criminal. But she didn't care at that moment.

She looked up at Angelo seductively and took him by the hand and led him to the bed. Angelo unbuttoned his shirt off of Riley and cupped her round breasts in his hands and lowered down to suck the left nipple until it was hard and pointed. As he suckled her tits, Riley slowly unzipped his slacks to reveal his manhood. It popped right out of his pants as if eager for some air. "Oh baby, you are as hard as steel," said Riley.

"Only for your beauty, my love," said Angelo. Riley immediately dropped to her knees and slowly took Angelo's penis into her hot and sultry mouth. She gulped and made swallowing sounds that drove Angelo wild. Riley ripped his pants down to his ankles and took his whole cock deep in her throat. She pushed him onto the bed and really went down hard on his huge Italian meat.

Riley deep throated Angelo ravenously. It surprised her that she was so hungry for cock. But this was no ordinary cock. It was the cock of the man she was falling for. It sounded crazy to Riley, but it was true.

There are real cases of love at first sight and Riley knew that was happening to her. Just then Angelo purred, "Come up here beside me, darling, and let me make love to you the way it should be done."

Riley lay down beside Angelo and he got on top of her gently and began to make sweet love to her. The room was a solid black by this time and Riley and Angelo relied only upon their senses as they made passionate, breathless love. It was a magical experience for the two of them. Their bodies were on fire, sliding with sweat against one another as their greedy mouths ravaged the other.

The sounds, the smells and the feel of their bodies grinding in exquisite ecstasy was unlike anything either of them had ever shared. It was as if they simply could not get enough of one another. They couldn't kiss hard enough, Angelo couldn't get his penis inside her deep enough, they couldn't groan loud enough.

"Angelo, I am in love with you," said Riley as she kissed him harder and more passionately than even before.

With a breathless voice Angelo whispered, "And I with you, baby. You are my dream woman. You are perfect for me." They rolled over without Angelo never removing himself from inside Riley's hot pussy. Riley rode Angelo slow and hard and ground her hips into his hair and his flesh. She arched her back slightly and came all over his pubic hair and his lap. Riley moaned with ecstasy that was filled with love and raw animal lust. She continued to bump and grind until she could feel his gigantic balls draw up to her soft ass. Then Angelo groaned loudly and consistently as the first spurt of cum gushed inside of her.

Then he paused and did it again and again.

This is what lovemaking is all about, thought Riley. If it isn't, I don't know what is.

(1 Month Later)

Riley and Angelo had been on the island almost three weeks, and it was a paradise like nothing they had ever dreamed of. They both were running for their freedom. Angelo was running from his old life in the mob. Riley was running from her old life as an agent for the FBI.

On the surface what they were doing seemed ludicrous, but they were more in love than they ever thought possible. After landing on a very remote island in the South Atlantic Ocean the others on the yacht were flown out of there sworn to keep Angelo's secret. He paid for them to start new lives in Europe.

Angelo had allies on the inside that helped them, but he was still in grave danger of being found and killed. He went against his dad, the Godfather. Trying to kill the guy who owed the mob and collecting the money for his gambling debt at the First National Bank had been a disaster.

On top of that one of Angelo's goons had fucked up and kidnapped Agent Riley Morgan of the FBI.

Now to make matters worse Angelo had found the love of his life and no longer wanted to be a killer. He never did. "Angelo, do you think we will survive?" said Riley. "Do you think they will find us here?"

"I don't know darling, but hopefully we... or I... can get out of here before they do."

"Angelo, why did you say I after you said we?"

"Because, Riley, I don't want you to give up your dreams and your career for a killer such as me," said Angelo.

"You WERE a killer. You aren't anymore," said Riley. "I weighed my choices and I cannot live without you my love," said Riley. "I am crazy about you and I am so in love with you."

"Riley, I can get you a helicopter out of here and you can go back to New York to the job that you love," said Angelo.

"No Angelo, I refuse to live without you. We're in this together okay?" replied Riley. Angelo held Riley's face in his hands and pulled her to him for a kiss.

"You are so beautiful Riley. I adore you baby."

"I am crazy about you, too, Angelo." "How about we go skinny dipping? It's almost twilight," said Riley.

Angelo laughed. "Of course, darling, anything you want," he replied.

Riley ran across the white sand beach nude and landed in the crystal blue water. Angelo watched her as she played and thought how lucky he was to have such a beautiful and devoted woman.

"Come on baby! The water is perfect," yelled Riley.

Angelo ran naked to the water where his dream woman swam and frolicked. They laughed and splashed and dunked one another. They were amazing together. As they walked out of the water they both plopped down on the sand holding one another face to face.

They started to kiss and, as always, once they started, it usually led to unbelievable lovemaking right there on the sand. This time was no different. Riley mounted Angelo and rode him slow right there in the moonlight. She looked almost like an angel with the stars dancing off of her blonde hair. The expression on her face as she fucked his hard penis was that of pure ecstasy. Angelo reached up and grasped one tit in each hand and twisted her nipples while she fucked him. He could tell his woman was about to come. She would sit straight up and close her eyes and throw her head back. That is exactly what happened the moment Angelo had the erotic thought.

As she started to cum for him he did as well at the same time. They became a tangled mass of orgasmic motion as they danced the dance of love with their bodies together on that secluded beach under the stars. These two knew that they had a crazy future ahead of them always looking over their shoulders, but they were bound and determined to be inseparable and hold one another up.

"Angelo I must admit I am scared about where our future lies." said Riley.

"I am too, darling, but together we can

conquer anything." said Angelo. "Tomorrow morning our plane will arrive and we will be on our way half way across the world. We will have new identities and new lives ahead of us." said Angelo. "Now let's go inside our tent and rest some before we take off on our big adventure." After getting inside and lying down, Riley asked Angelo to hold her tight and he did until they both drifted off into a peaceful sleep.

The next morning, Riley and Angelo were startled awake by the noise of several helicopters overhead. "Oh my God," said Riley. "They've found us. What will we do Angelo?" Riley whispered hysterically.

Angelo had a very worried look upon his face. "Calm down Riley and let's think. I will see if our plane is anywhere near here and, darling, if it is we will just have to run for it. I will give you a gun for protection Riley. I know you can use it if need be."

The sounds of the helicopters were getting lower and suddenly they heard a voice say "This is the FBI please step out of the tent." Then Riley heard a familiar voice, it was her partner Joe Barillo. He was yelling through the hand held speaker. "Riley Morgan are you in there? Let me know by coming out. We can help you, Riley." said Joe. Riley broke down in tears for the first time since she was a cop she was truly frightened of getting shot or seeing the man she loved shot down.

Just then Riley and Angelo heard his plane flying overhead. Angelo radioed for them to land a mile or so away so he and Riley could escape. Angelo looked at Riley and said:

"Okay baby are you ready? Once we go out the back, we will have to run like hell to make it to the plane. Remember what we practiced in our training right?"

"Yes I remember," said Riley.

"Okay, we have out bullet proof vests, our guns, ammunition and radios." said Angelo. "Give me a kiss darling. I love you with all my heart Riley."

"I love you too Angelo. We can do this," said Riley.

They grabbed each other's hand and took off full speed ahead towards their destination. As they ran swiftly, they could hear all sorts of noise overhead, but it didn't stop Riley and Angelo from their dreams of a life together - albeit it a hard life. They would have one another and to them that really was all that mattered.

At one point, Angelo plunged forward and fell down it sounded as if he had been shot and Riley's heart almost stopped, but Angelo got up again and kept running with the woman he loved by his side. They ran harder and faster until just up ahead they could see their plane. Would they make it out of here in time?

"Good morning darling. How did you sleep?" said Angelo as he looked at his beautiful woman asleep on the airplane. Riley looked around a bit confused and then smiled at

Angelo and said:

"Oh baby, we made it! We're here together on a plane headed for... where did you say we were headed for?" giggled Riley.

"That is a surprise and you will just have to wait a bit longer to find out, but I assure you, Riley, you are going to love it!" Angelo replied.

"Come on baby tell me just a little hint please pretty please," said Riley.

"Riley you cannot make me say anything! Ok?" Angelo could hardly resist Riley when she became insistent. Riley took her pillow from behind her head and started to bop Angelo over the head with it playfully. Angelo grabbed her face just then and gave her a long, passionate kiss that said he adored her. Then Angelo said "Close your eyes darling," said Angelo.

"Why?" asked Riley. "Because there is one surprise I am willing to let you see if you want to," said Angelo. Riley closed her eyes and Angelo took her hand in his and then said, "Okay you can open those beautiful blue eyes now." When Riley opened her eyes, she saw the most beautiful sapphire and diamond ring she had ever laid eyes on.

"Oh Angelo it is dazzling. Thank you," said Riley.

"Not nearly as dazzling as you are my love." Then Angelo got down on one knee right there on the plane and said, "Riley Morgan will you do me Angelo Russo the honor of being my wife?" and he slipped the ring upon Riley's finger.

Riley began to cry and said in a small voice, "Yes, yes yes I will," and she and Angelo hugged and kissed and sealed their love. Soon they would be landing in a new location and headed for a new life. Would they be able to stand strong together and not get caught? Could their love conquer the odds that lie ahead of them?

4 GUILTY FIRES OF PASSION

Frank Murphy got up early every morning and did his daily workout. Then, headed out for the day, checking on his family and friends, reading, writing, and doing his art. His paintings were the most important thing in the world to Frank, besides God and his family, of course. Frank was a very devout Catholic and never missed mass, or doing his daily prayers to the rosary. Frank was 56 years old and amazingly handsome and in shape for his age. Frank was born and raised in the volatile country of Ireland, and was all too familiar with hard times and oppression.

Frank had been married for 20 years and had two grown children. He and his wife, Bernadette, had been divorced for 5 years now. After the divorce, Frank took the opportunity to move to the states with his job.

A former police detective, he moved to New York City to head up a special crimes unit for them, but had since retired from the force, about a year ago. Frank gathered his supplies in his art bag and headed toward Second Street, to the old abandoned building that was now used for their art classes.

Frank mad it to his art class, just in time to get there and get set up with his easel and his supplies. He has enrolled in an advanced class this time, which meets three times a week. Frank's style was to paint and draw very simple lines and figures. He hd even dabbled in a bit of modern and contemporary art forms. Frank was busy at work and he had a few quick hellos with the girl to his left named Brandy. She was a pretty girl, but too young and not exactly Frank's type. He had an on and off again relationship with a woman in Connecticut, but nothing too serious. They had met online, in an art forum. But it was nearly impossible, as far as Frank could see, trying to carry on a long distance relationship.

As Frank was preparing his paint and brushes, and he heard a rustling to his left. He looked up and his jaw about hit the floor, but, of course, he kept a straight face all the while. Frank was looking at a gorgeous red head that, for some reason, sparked his interest immediately. Frank was already questioning himself. Frank had been mostly with brunettes, but there was something about this fiery woman, who was unpacking her art bag, that unleashed a fire within Frank that disturbed him, to say the least. He pulled his eyes away from her glorious hair and body, and got back to his own project, knowing full well he was captivated, immediately.

Frank was busying himself when he hear a voice from his left say, "Excuse me sir, do they provide us with any extra tools or supplies here, since we did pay so much for this class?"

Frank looked over and saw her beautiful face, with a sprinkling of freckles and a smile that would light up midnight. "I am sorry, ma'am, what did you say?" asked Frank.

She repeated the question and gave him a seductive giggle at the end. "Oh, forgive me, my name is Colette Colton. Nice to meet you, uh, what did you say your name was?" She said.

"Oh, I didn't. My name is Frank." He said, flashing his gorgeous smile.

"Okay then, hi Frank, nice to meet you." Colette said, extending her hand. A wave of fire ran through Frank's body, as he squeezed Colette's soft, warm hand.

What is wrong with you Frank? he thought to himself.

Colette also felt an amazing connection between her and Frank. Sparks and tingly sensations ran through every cell of her body, as they touched.

"Is this class hard? How's the instructor?" Asked Colette. Just then, Brandy, from Frank's right side, chimed in. "Frank is a very serious artist and likes to keep private. He doesn't talk much." said Brandy, with obvious venom in her voice.

"For your information, he spoke to me first. So, if you would mind your business, I'd appreciate it," retorted Colette.

Frank smiled inside, thinking, My God, what a little Firecracker she is! Then, he found himself thinking what her copper red hair would look like between his legs, sucking his cock, which was getting increasingly harder by the minute.

"Am I bothering you much, Frank?" said Colette, with innocent green eyes and, yet, a seductive look that would set a man on fire.

"No, you are fine, Colette, and quite a talented artist." Frank replied.

"Thank you, Frank," said Colette, laying a wet kiss on his left cheek. "You are a real sweetie pie," she said, flashing her emerald eyes at him.

Frank was feeling all sorts of things for this woman and he really had no idea why. She was unlike anyone he had ever met before and simply stunning, as well. They talked on and off for the entirety of their art class.

When it came time to leave class, Frank watched Colette, along with each and every graceful move that her body made. God, she was gorgeous and uninhibited. Frank could feel his cock tingle in his pants, and feel them tighten a bit around it. He felt a surge of guilt, also, swirl inside his mind. He knew better than to let petty temptation flavor his thoughts. He was supposed to be committed to his girlfriend, Janet, but Colette was pulling on his emotions like a tempestuous storm.

Never before, in his life, had Frank experienced such raging passion and emotion for another person. Suddenly, Frank was startled back into reality by a voice behind him.

"See you Wednesday, Frank," said Colette, smiling seductively, yet, innocently. "Maybe we can show up early and you can show me some of those sketches you were telling me about."

"You could drop by my apartment tomorrow morning, if you'd like," said Frank, who was also asking himself why one earth he just said that.

He was 56 years old, Colette's senior by at least 20 years. Actually, he was 21 years older than Colette. Colette was 35 years old.

"Sure, I'd love to." Said Colette, flashing a smile that would light up the entire world, thought Frank. Frank jotted down his address, for Colette, and he left out for his walk home, but first, he would stop by the church for a quick prayer.

Frank walked through the door of his apartment, about an hour later, feeling ambiguous inside, at best. He felt contrition in his heart and passion in his loins for this amazing woman that stormed through his life like a dark torrent. Frank decided he needed a shower to cool his thoughts, and his loins.

Frank was a very handsome and virile man.

Women everywhere flocked to him and begged to be his girl, but it wasn't an easy thing to get the attention of Frank. He was in great physical shape and he had elegant, classy looks that drove women wild. He also had a smile that would light up any room.

Frank hopped in the shower and let the water flow down his back, like a trickling waterfall. There he stood, the bar of soap in his hand, as he circled his cock and balls with it, making a soapy froth that made his shaft tighten and the head so sensitive. Reaching down with his right hand, he took the greasy shaft in his firm grip and pulled the skin away from him slowly, in a series of soapy strokes that had Frank's cock straining to be pulled even faster. Each pass of his hand along its length made it stiffen further as his clenched fingers bumped across the swollen pink head, making his legs tremble as he tried to stand with his back arched, thrusting his cock forward, as if begging her to suck it, while she kneeled before him in the hot pounding water, in the tub.

His eyes were closed, picturing Colette's mouth closing around his cockhead and sucking it deep inside her mouth, while her hand cupped his huge, cum filled balls gently, feeling each of his nuts slipping around in her soapy palm as she pulled and sucked on his cock head, her other hand stroking the length of his slippery shaft. Suddenly, Frank felt her sucking stop and he opened his eyes to see Colette lying back against the tub before him, her legs spread, while she held her left tit to her mouth and she sucked her long hard nipple. Her other hand was furious in her crotch, first plunging three fingers inside her pussy, making sucking and juicy sounds, before she pulled them out and quickly rubbed her clit, while watching Frank's hand return to his cock and milk the shaft slowly. Colette could see the pink head of his cock peeking out, from the end of his fingers and she moaned, her fingers pulling on her long lips and frantically fucking her creamy cunt in rapid succession. Frank could see that your pussy was so close to cumming, it made him stroke his cock harder and faster. He could feel the cum, so urgent in his balls, to splash out and cover her face as she finger fucked herself to a huge orgasm on the floor of the tub, in front of him.

Suddenly, Frank knew it was time. He watched her ass come up off the tub, as she took her hand away from her pussy, to allow the sudden splash of her cum to squirt up towards him. Frank pointed his soapy, lathered cock and hand towards her, as she saw his cream spew forth and land on her face. Frank straddled her tits and watched the first squirt land directly in Colette's mouth, and each one thereafter, coating her face with a thick creaminess. He gently pulled on the electrically charged head of his still drooling cock, as the soap and his cum mixed together in his hand. Her hand reached up to take his and feel his cock still twitching in both their grasps. Colette's fingers gently swirled around the pebbly ridges of Frank's cock rim. She saw his hips jerk, as she teased his gradually shrinking cock. The water was hot, but Frank made it hotter, tipping his head back and closing his eyes to feel the steaming hot streams soothing his soul, while his heart still pounded loudly in his chest...

Frank got out of the shower and towelled off his pulsating body, wishing that what he had just dreamed was true and, on the other hand, feeling guilty as hell that he was masturbating, thinking of a virtual stranger. What was it about Colette that set his mind and body in flames? He wasn't sure, but he had a feeling he had better get a handle on it before it grew into a fevered mass of passionate lust. Frank went to his bedroom and prayed his rosary, feeling contrite and saddened. Frank drifted off to sleep, finally, and dreamed seductive dreams of Colette all night long.

The next morning, Frank awoke and the first thought on his mind with this gorgeous redhead that seemed to be taking over each and every thought he had ever had. He quickly remembered that Colette would be stopping by in about an hour. So, Frank scurried around, straightening up a few things here and there. He lit a scented candle and put on some soft jazz in the background.

Why are you doing this Frank? he asked himself once more. Are you nuts?

He then went to his art room and fetched the sketches that he had spoken to Colette about. As he was thumbing through them remembering things about when he had sketched them he heard the buzzer. It was the redheaded beauty, now.

Frank went, quietly and peacefully, to the door and opened it up to the vision standing before him. "Hi, Frankie!" said Colette, with a wide grin on her beautiful face. "Do you mind if I call you that?" She whisked into the room like a ray of sunshine.

"Well, usually only my family calls me that, but you can if you like." Said Frank. "Thanks sweetie," she said, as she laid a big sloppy kiss on his cheek, sending waves of excitement through his body. "Let's go sit down on the sofa and I'll show you those sketches. Would you care for something to drink? Some iced tea, a cola, or a glass of wine perhaps?" asked Frank.

"I'd love a glass of wine!" said Colette. "Very well, I'll go grab us a couple of glasses," said Frank.

Colette was enamored with this elegant and intriguing man. She had to admit he made her tingle all over and get warm in all of the right places. She found him to be handsome, charming, and sexy as hell.

Frank came back with their chardonnay and said, "Here you go lovely lady."

"Thank you Frankie," said Colette. As Frank showed Colette his many sketches and explained them to her, she leaned in, very close to him, to see. As she leaned into him, he noticed how divine she smelled. He could also feel her pointed nipples up against his arm. This drove him wild with desire for this foxy redhead sitting on his couch. She was so full of fire and passion. He could see it, feel it, and so badly wanted to drink it.

Colette could feel that Frank wanted her and she wanted him just as badly. She could smell the musk of his cologne. She could also see the longing in his eyes when she looked at him. Before either of them knew what hit them, they found themselves involved in a ravenous kiss that caught them by surprise. The feelings between them were so electric that it tingled down both of their bodies and sent goose bumps all over them.

Frank kissed Colette with a vehement fervor that he didn't even realize resided within him. He hungered for every inch and every drop of her. He desired to drink every delicious drop of her sweet, ambrosial delights and then some.

"I want to drink from your cup," Frank said in a heated tone that set Colette's body aflame. Frank got on his knees in front of Colette and raised her sundress up to her hips, revealing her beautiful fiery red flower. It had a patch of copper red hair on it, hiding two luscious pink lips that Frank could not wait to devour in his hungry mouth.

"Your pussy is so beautiful and delectable," Frank said, looking up at Colette with raw animal lust and some love that would soon come to be.

"Eat my pussy Frankie. Please devour every drop of my juice," said Colette, in a seductive tone that made Frank's cock swell huge in his pants.

Colette pushed Frank's head down between

her milky white thighs. She gasped when he latched onto her horny pussy lips. He suckled each lip, one at a time, pulling them ever so tenderly through his mouth, making Colette shudder with ecstasy. She could feel the heat rise in her body, from the tips of her toes to the top of her beautiful red mane.

Frank continued to feast on Colette's pussy, fiercely moving his head back and forth, devouring every last delicious drop of it. Colette grabbed Frank's face and said, "Frank, make love to me, NOW." That's all Frank needed to hear. He was so horny to get inside of her beautiful flower.

Frank reached out for Colette's hand and said, "Come on, let's go to my bed, where we can make love in comfort." Colette didn't say a word, but allowed Frank to lead her to his bed. Once in the bedroom, Frank unzipped Colette's dress and let it fall softly to the ground. Colette unzipped Frank's pants, revealing his swollen cock inside. Frank took her face in his hands and kissed her with mad passion, unlike any kiss Colette had ever received. Frank laid Colette upon his bed and entered her from the missionary position. He pulled his raging cock in and out of her in excruciatingly slow moves that caused Colette to shudder with pure ecstasy each, and every, time his member slipped out of her and dared to go back inside.

Colette ground her hips upward, towards Frank's cock, as he plunged deeper and harder still. He lavished Colette with kisses on her neck, freckled shoulders, and down her beautiful arms. He took in the aroma of her flesh, desiring to breathe in every intoxicating scent of her moistened skin. He craved her like he had never craved another woman in his life. She craved him like she had never craved another man in her life.

"Colette, I want to have every inch of you. I am going to shoot my cum inside of you, baby," he said.

"I am going to cum all over your cock, too, Frankie," said Colette.

At that time, the two of them rocked their bodies in a seductive and orgasmic motion that set their flesh on fire. They both reached the peak of orgasm at the same time. It felt as though their bodies melted into one another's. It also felt as if the orgasmic surge would never end. Frank did not want to remove his throbbing muscle from inside Colette. Her pussy had a strong grip on it, as well. The two of them lay there basking in the warmth of the passion that resided between them. They both longed for this moment to never end. Gently, they fell asleep as Frank's cock resided in Colette's hot pussy for the remainder of the afternoon, until, as it softened, it gently slipped out of her wet, moist snatch.

Late that afternoon, Frank and Colette woke up kind of startled to find that they were intertwined in an embrace. They were face to face, looking into each other's eyes. "You are so lovely, Colette. You are such a Firecracker in bed!" Frank said, smiling. "Do you know that you could lead me into all sorts of temptations that I don't need to be involved in. I have a girlfriend, Colette. She lives in Connecticut," he said, sadly.

"Frankie, are you going to lie there and tell me that you don't feel the spark between us? Are you going to dare tell me that you don't feel the raging passion between us? It is beyond our control Frankie. Why don't you just enjoy it?" said Colette.

"You make it sound so easy, Colette. This is just lust between us and you know that," said Frank.

Colette's eyes grew a fiery deep green. "How can you say that to me, Frank? Did you not feel what I felt here today?" she replied.

"We have to squelch this between us, Colette, before we get too wrapped up in it. I am a Christian man and I have God to consider," said Frank.

"What are you saying, Frankie? Are you saying I am the devil's seed?" replied Colette.

Frankie smiled. "Boy you are a little Firecracker, aren't you?" She just looked at him with hurt in her eyes. Then, Colette got up, threw her sundress on, grabbed her things, and left in a huff.

Frank lay there for a long while thinking about the incredible lovemaking that he had just shared with Colette. She was right and Frank knew it, but he didn't want to admit it. The incredible feeling of guilt took Frank's mind over. He was torn between his devotion to the church, his girlfriend, and the amazing passion he felt for Colette. He was afraid that he may never truly be able to enjoy the fire that was raging inside Colette and the obvious passion she felt for him. He was afraid he would just be left with a dark torrent of longing and yearning. He had no desire to hurt Colette. He couldn't explain the connection between them, but he had to agree with her, there definitely was something beyond either of their power going on.

The next day, Frank was already setting up his workspace and dabbing at his painting when Colette arrived, just a few minutes before art class began. "Good morning, Firecracker," said Frank, to the fiery redhead that stood looking at him, as if to say go to hell. "Cute, Frank, real cute," said Colette, with blazing green eyes, looking straight at Frank.

"Ouch, that burned, you hot little number," said Frank under his breath.

Then, Brandy chimed in, "Frank, is she interrupting your delicate genius, again?" Before Frank had time to answer, he noticed Colette walking over to Brandy's workspace. "

Uh-oh," thought Frank. This could get ugly.

"Hey! Watch it. Okay? Keep your nose out of my fucking business. Got it, Miss Sunshine?"

Frank was trying to contain his laughter, but Colette heard a bit of a giggle coming from his direction.

"What's so fucking funny, Frankie?" said Colette, in a growl.

"Golly Frank, she's a real lady of rage, isn't she?" said Brandy. They both laughed and Colette was pissed enough to spit bullets.

Colette made it through the rest of the class without ripping anyone's eyes out, but it wasn't easy. Colette was the first to admit that she had a wicked temper. When the art class was dismissed, Colette quickly gathered her belongings and tore out of there like a tornado. Frank was left in her whirlwind, wondering how on earth to contain this Firecracker. Colette took off walking pretty fast, but soon enough, Frank was able to catch her.

"Slow down you hot thing." Said Frank. "Why are you so hot under the collar?"

"You know good and damn well why I am so pissed," said Colette. "First of all, you fuck me, then, you practically throw me out of your bed... and then, that little bitch this morning was all over you."

Just then, Frank grabbed Colette and kissed her like a wild man full of passion for her. Colette was still trying to speak, but Frank kept kissing her, until she gave into the passion and kissed him back.

"Frankie, take me to your house and make love to me, right now," said Colette.

"Sure thing, beautiful. Come on," said Frank.

On the walk over to his apartment, Frank was riddled with guilty flames of passion in his gut. But, he was also consumed with the yearning and longing for Colette that he had racing throughout every pore in his body.

When they reached Frank's apartment, the two of them barely got inside the door before they were ripping each other's clothes off and kissing ravenously. Colette unbuttoned her skirt and let it fall to the ground, revealing her panty less, red pussy. Frank nearly gasped at the sight of her standing there. Then, she reached inside her bag and pulled out her favorite purple toy.

"Do you want to see me make my pussy cum, Frankie?" asked Colette.

"Yes darling, make it spill to the floor. Let me see that hot pussy cum," answered Frank. Colette started using the vibe on her clit and making her cookie feel so fucking good. She plunged it in and out of her, driving her snatch crazy with horny desire.

She could hardly take it anymore, so she got on the floor and spread her legs out wide open, revealing to Frank her meaty, turned on pussy, while she played with it, hard and fast. She had one foot on the coffee table and one on the chair. So, she was spread eagle in front of him. Frank could not help but want to feast on the vision before his eyes.

"Baby, you look intoxicating. Can I eat you out?" he asked.

"No way, you have to watch in agony while I make myself cum,l" said Colette. Colette started rubbing her snatch fervently, and faster than ever, and she focused mainly on her protruding clit head.

As she vibrated her clit, it became hot pink with desire and started producing a creamy cum that made Frank so fucking thirsty for her cum in his mouth. He pulled out his dick and started wanking it, full throttle. Colette arched her back and start thrashing, ready to squirt her red pussy everywhere. "Oh fuck, that feels so damn good," said Colette, as her squirt sprayed out of her slick pussy.

Just then, frank shot a wad of cum over Colette's head hitting her face and hair.

Then, his throbbing member shot two more loads of spunk in a row, making Frank nearly howl with desire and sheer lust. Then, Frank suddenly placed Colette's feet behind her ears and started banging her hard and furious. You could hear his massive balls popping her ass, as Frank thrust in and out of her furry snatch. Suddenly, Colette felt his balls draw tight and his cock got rigid, like a pole inside her, and Frank shot again, straight up inside her cunt.

Frank collapsed beside Colette and held her for what seemed like hours. There was something like kismet going on between these two, but neither of them understood it and they were both really afraid of it. They knew that they possessed a passionate fire between them and that it could be a dangerous flame, if not kept watch of.

Later that evening, Colette had to get back home. Some nights she had to babysit her nephew for her sister. This was one of those nights. "So, I guess I'll see you tomorrow at art class?" asked Colette.

"Yes," said Frankie, very quietly.

"What's wrong my Irish dream man?" asked Colette.

"Oh nothing, Colette. I just feel torn and I also feel so much guilt about falling into this affair with you. I think you are an amazing and passionate woman, who I could easily love, but I do have a girlfriend and I have my faith," said Frank. "I cannot help but feel it is wrong what we are doing."

"How can you say that? You know very well there is a spark and a force between us that is special and very rare, Frankie." answered Colette.

"Yes, there is, Colette. I agree," said Frank. "Just go on home and take care of your nephew. We'll talk tomorrow."

Colette was not very happy with Frank's quick response to her concerns, but she did have to get back home. So, she left without a kiss goodbye, or anything.

Frank felt terrible about how things were transpiring between him and Colette. He adored every inch of her and craved her even more. He simply did not know how he could live without her. She was that important to him for some unknown reason, but Frank, unfortunately, knew what he must do if he wanted to be free from the guilty fires that roared within him.

First of all, Frank walked to the church and prayed his rosary and got on his face before the Lord. He prayed that he was making the right choice for both he and Colette. That night, Frank actually wept himself to sleep. He was truly beginning to fall in love with Colette.

The next day, Colette rushed to get ready for art class. She was extremely anxious to see Frankie. Yes, he was extremely stubborn and very mysterious, but she was crazy about him and he lit her fire like no other man ever could. She dressed in a scarlet red sundress to please Frankie. He loved it when she wore red. He called her his Firecracker and Colette adored that so much.

When Colette arrived at the art studio she was very surprised to see that Frank wasn't at his work station setting up his paints and easel. When she got to her station she noticed a piece of paper tucked underneath some of the supplies. It looked like a note. Colette opened up the note that read:

Dear Firecracker,

I know you must be wondering, about now, what is going on and why you are reading this note. I had to make some tough choices Colette. I know this is going to be very difficult for you to accept, but please try to understand. I know that deep in your heart you do. You know that I pride myself on being an honest man and a spiritual man. You also know that I have a girlfriend who is counting on me to be truthful to her. I could no longer, in good conscience, do this to her, Firecracker. You are a vibrant, smart, and beautiful woman. You deserve someone that can return the love that you have to give. I am sorry, Colette, but that someone isn't me. You are a radiant flower that deserves to shine in the sunlight. The passion and fire between us, my darling, was beautiful and I will never forget it. Believe me, you will be in my thoughts for a long time to come. I am also moving, Colette, so don't try to find me. We had our few good times, let's remember it that way. Please accept my choice.

Colette was too emotionally distraught to stay in art class, so she left quietly and went home. She cried rivers of tears over Frankie. She was so hurt and confused and couldn't believe what was happening to her.

Colette hardly left her house for two weeks, but when she did she was frantically looking for Frankie everywhere. She searched everywhere, even online, and nothing. He had simply disappeared.

One day, Colette's best friend, Diana, brought over an ad for a new art class starting up, not far from where Colette lived, but a bit further than the other one she had attended, by Frankie broke her heart. Colette decided she would sign up and go to the class.

She got showered and dressed and headed out towards the new studio. Little did Colette know, Frankie had been keeping a close eye on his treasure, Colette. Boy, did she look beautiful tonight. He felt so guilty for hurting her tender heart.

When Colette got to her work station, she could swear she smelled Frankie's cologne, but she finally decided she must be imagining it. She did see a sketch on her desk and she wondered who it belonged to. She looked at it and the lines seemed very familiar, somehow. By the time class was over, Colette was beginning to feel rather sad.

She left class and headed down the street with thoughts of Frankie swirling through her mind.

Colette was walking along, lost in her own little world, when she heard a gentle, sexy Irish voice behind her. "Hello, Firecracker. You look absolutely exquisite this evening."

She turned around to see Frankie's gorgeous smile looking into her green eyes.

She wrapped her arms around him and said, "I am in love with you, Frankie."

He held her face in his hands and said, "I am in love with you, as well, Firecracker, and I simply cannot deny anymore." Frankie kissed Colette right there, in the middle of 9th street, with beautiful autumn leaves falling all around them. The passionate fire that resided between Colette and Frank could never be put out. It was beyond their control, or understanding.

5 PASSIONATE ADVANTAGES

Allie and Zak had been inseparable since they met in high school. Allie remembers the day she met Zak just like it was yesterday. She had just moved to the big city of Houston, Texas, with her mom and dad from a small one-horse town. Allie was extremely shy the first day she stepped foot onto the campus of Houston Central High School.

She was scared as she made her way through the halls trying to make it to her locker. Finally, she found her locker number 2B. She was putting her books away in the drab gray compartment when she heard Zak's voice for the first time, saying, "Hi is this your first day here?" Allie looked up and saw the most handsome guy she had ever laid eyes on.

"My name is Zak. What's your name?"

"I'm Allie."

"Nice to meet you Allie; allow me to show you around campus," as he offered his hand for her to take.

As Allie and Zak finished out their last two years of high school, Allie carries a secret torch for Zak that she simply cannot extinguish. She and Zak were best friends, but to everyone else, it seemed like nothing more. Only Allie knew how head over heels in love with Zak she was, at least that's what she thought. Deep down, Zak Freemont was crazy about Allie Sommers as well.

Even though he didn't let her know it, he thought she was absolutely the most exciting and awesome girl he had ever met. There was something about Allie that drove Zak wild! Even though she was a bookworm and the quiet type, he knew deep down there was a tiger just waiting to roar inside Allie.

Zak never let on to Allie that he felt that way; his friends on the football team would have ribbed him for years over that. Zak dated Tina, the head cheerleader. Sure Tina was blonde, blue eyed, and smokin' hot, but she wasn't what ignited Zak's passion.

Throughout the remainder of high school and up until the day they admitted it to one another, Allie Sommers and Zak Freemont were both head over heels in love with each other, and they didn't even know the other one felt this way.

Allie was so excited she could hardly contain herself! Her very best friend Zak would be at her house any minute. She hadn't seen Zak in over two years! Zak was something of a daredevil and had joined the Marines out of high school not long after the tragedy of 9-11 happened, and Zak had been deployed to the Middle East.

Allie remembered the day they stood in the airport tears rolling down their cheeks, locked together in a tight embrace. She truly thought that she might never see her best friend ever again. Zak was brave and had served his country with dignity and honor. Knowing this made Allie love Zak even more. She didn't think that was possible.

Allie had tried numerous relationships, but none of them lit a fire in her like Zak. Allie wondered would she ever be able to tell Zak how she truly felt. She had her day to day 8 to 4 job as an elementary school teacher in Houston, and Zak was out fighting back enemies. The two of them were opposites for sure.

Just then Allie was startled back from her daydream by a few knocks at the door. It must be Zak!

Allie ran to the door flung it open, and before either of them could say a word, Zak swept her off her feet and twirled her around and they hugged and embraced. Once they were finally able to stop hugging, Zak gently lowered Allie to the ground and stood back to look at her. She was breathtaking, Zak thought. Her hair was still the strawberry blonde mass of curls that had driven him wild with desire for these past years. Her eyes still had that hazel spark that twinkled every time she looked at him. Her body was still the drop dead gorgeous body he so badly wanted and needed.

"You look hot baby!" Zak said with a wink and a smile that showed off his adorable dimples.

"You don't look too shabby yourself," replied Allie. My God was he ever a massive hunk of tanned muscle, a head full of gorgeous blonde hair, and he had a smile that could melt you like butter, thought Allie to herself. She couldn't help but feel the slight erection he had underneath his jeans as he was spinning her around in that exciting embrace. Allie must admit it made her feel a bit tingly inside, and it aroused thoughts in her that she probably shouldn't be having.

"Come on inside, and I'll get you a cold beer," Allie said. "I bet you could use one after that long trip."

"Boy could I ever," said Zak.

Allie walked to the kitchen and grabbed them a couple of beers out of the fridge and hurried back to sit by Zak on the sofa.

As she sat down with Zak and began to pop the tab of her beer, Zak said, "So how have you been Princess?" (This was a name Zak has lovingly called her since right after they met). "Anything new in the love department?" Allie knew he would ask her, and she dreaded telling him what had been going on. It was a humiliating experience, and she truly didn't want to talk about it. But she knew Zak was very persistent and would never give up, so she decided she may as well be honest.

"My love life isn't going too well at all Zak. I made some really stupid choices, and now, I am paying for them with a shattered heart and a wounded pride." Allie said as she looked down at her throw pillow with the frayed edge that she loved to play with when she got nervous. "Did somebody hurt you Princess? Because if they did...."

"Zak! It is okay nothing for you to worry about! I just recently broke up with a man I had been seeing for nearly 10 months now. It was devastating for me, that's all, and humiliating."

"What is it Allie?" Zak replied in a tender voice. "You can tell me anything."

Before she realized it, Allie had unloaded the whole sordid story on her best friend who had just gotten back from the Middle East. Allie felt bad she put all of this on Zak's shoulders. As Allie said the words out loud, she couldn't believe how stupid she had been to fall for Justin's façade. Justin was the man that Allie had foolishly fallen for online. Allie had been lonely about a year ago after another failed relationship with a guy named Brandon, and she was feeling very vulnerable that night she signed online. Allie had always been seen as a prude or the shy type, so that night, she decided to do something she had never done before. She went onto a dating site called Hot Hookups.com and made a profile.

This was totally out of Allie's character, but she was sick and tired of being the good girl and getting dumped. This is when she met Justin. He wooed Allie with his charming ways and his poetic style. He proclaimed his true and devotion love to her. Allie was completely swept off her feet until the day she just happened to be on one of the major search engines searching a term for her students. Something in her search brought up something familiar to Allie. It took her a few minutes to figure it out, but suddenly it hit her. The name that came up on one of the links was a nickname that she had remembered Justin telling her about. It was his nickname on an "old" chat site he used to be a member of. With a little bit of investigation, Allie was able to put the pieces together.

To make a long story short, the man who said he was "so in love with her," Justin, wasn't in love with her at all. He was a heartless player, and worse than that, Justin was a married man! Allie was floored when she saw that eye-opening fact came up on her screen just a few short months before. As the memory of that night came flooding back now, Allie was overtaken with emotion. She couldn't contain the flood of tears filling her eyes.

"Oh Zak," Allie cried, "I am so stupid! How could I fall for such a phony like Justin? I swear I will never trust another man again!"

"Don't worry about it babe, that idiot Justin doesn't know what a great girl he's missing out on. He's a loser Allie. Forget the low life. You can do much better than a jerk like that."

"All I attract are liars and cheaters Zak!" Allie sobbed.

"Come here," said Zak as he outstretched his strong comforting arms. Allie laid her head on Zak's chest and sobbed tears of regret and sorrow.

After Allie's tears dissipated, she found herself enjoying the arms of Zak. The smell of his sweater revealing the cologne he had worn since she met him. The strength of his arms around her felt wonderful. The sound of his heart in his chest made Allie feel like she had never felt before. She felt like she belonged right where she was, in the arms of the man she secretly adored.

Zak looked down at Allie whose head rest on his chest. He couldn't help but think how gorgeous she looked with her red curls in a tousle. He couldn't resist the urge to run his fingers through her soft tresses. He stroked her hair and then made his way down to her tense shoulders.

"Want me to rub ya?" asked Zak.

Allie looked up at Zak with tear-streaked cheeks, and Zak thought to himself that she had never looked sexier or more desirable than she did at this very moment. "Sure I'll let ya!" Allie smiled full well knowing that Zak Freemont gave the very best shoulder massages in the world.

Allie scooted into Zak, so he could reach her shoulders. He started to knead her tense flesh through her blouse, and it felt wonderfully relaxing. "Mmmmmmm," moaned Allie. "That feels so good."

The sound of her moaning like that always got Zak a little worked up in the hard-on department. "Does it now?" he whispered sexily into Allie's ear.

A whisper that sent goose bumps straight down Allie's spine to the tips of her toes. As she eased back further into Zak's muscular body Allie could feel the beginnings of arousal in Zak's pants. She tried to ignore it but that wasn't possible. She found herself only wanting to scoot closer into him so that she could feel the bulging mound right up next to her hot ass.

"Why don't you slip your blouse off so I can massage you better," Zak said in a sexy voice that made Allie tingle and feel warm all over.

"Ok, if you insist," replied Allie.

"Let me help you off with that," said Zak.

So Allie turned to face him as Zak unbuttoned one button after another, teasingly slow. As he neared the last button Allie looked up at Zak with desire in her eyes. Her hazel eyes sparkled with that familiar glimmer that drove Zak wild. They didn't say a word, but they both knew what was going on between them. The passionate sparks filled the room like a fireworks display.

As Zak unbuttoned the last button, he took his hands and slipped the silky blouse off of Allie's shoulders, revealing her lacy near see-through crème-colored bra. Through the lace, Zak could see pale pink nipples bulging against the lace. It was very obvious that Allie was aroused. Zak took his hands and cupped Allie's angelic face in them and pulled her into his hungry mouth. Zak and Allie started to kiss slowly and passionately. Those slow, wet kisses turned into ravenous and greedy kisses of lust, love, desire, and raw sex, all rolled up into one delicious and extremely hot kiss. They were both seething for the other one's body by this time.

Allie felt like being a bad girl, and in her most erotic and tantalizing voice said to Zak, "I want to get fucked, and I want you to fuck me right now!"

That did it, thought Zak, and he said, "You want me to fuck your hot pussy baby?"

Zak pulled Allie into his body even closer. Allie could feel the massive erection in his pants. Allie felt on fire inside for Zak. He passionately kissed her neck sending shock waves down her spine. Allie reached and stroked his manhood on top of his jeans. Zak let out a sensual groan that told Allie he wanted to be inside of her.

"Want to go to my bedroom?" Allie said seductively. Zak didn't say a word, but his eyes said it all. They smoldered with longing and desire. Zak gently took Allie's hand just like he had done on the first day they met and led her to her bedroom.

Once inside the bedroom, Allie stood before Zak and removed her bra and shorts. Zak couldn't believe how beautiful she looked standing nude before him. Her skin so soft and smooth, and the moonlight dancing off her copper curls as it shone through the window took Zak's breath away. He motioned for Allie to come lay down beside him.

Zak then began to kiss up and down Allie's body tenderly and erotically. The smell of her skin was like a sweet mixture of honeysuckle and jasmine, Zak thought. Zak slowly licked up Allie's smooth tummy all the way to her lips. Allie moaned with pleasure, causing Zak's hard on to expand even more. Allie reached down and stroked his throbbing cock. He felt so full and amazing in her hand as she stroked a bit of pre-cum from the head. Zak groaned with pleasure as he moved up to Allie's mouth and kissed her with tenderness and vehemence. Allie's nails scratched down Zak's back practically begging him to enter her. She craved his penis inside her more than she ever had craved anything in her entire life. Her pussy was drenched with juices just waiting for Zak to slip inside.

As Zak entered Allie, it felt as though their bodies melted into one another. Zak could feel Allie's full meaty pussy lips grab his cock with a grip that wasn't letting go anytime soon. No words were spoken. They spent for what seemed like an eternity moving to the rhythm of their ignited bodies. They kissed passionately and their bodies were slick with sweat. The musky yet alluring scent of sex filled the room.

After the most perfect lovemaking session, either of them had ever experienced, Allie and Zak collapsed onto the bed in total amazement at what the two of them had just shared. They looked at each other with a realization that something rare existed between them.

Without a word, Allie and Zak knew that they were madly in love and always would be.

As the sun peeked through the sheer curtains of Allie's bedroom the next morning, Allie started to wake up from a dreamy state she was in. She half opened one eye and let out a little early morning groan. Then suddenly, it dawned on her, and her hazel eyes opened wide. She was lying on Zak's hairy chest and could hear his heart beat in her right ear. She could smell the intoxicating aroma of lovemaking still lingering on the sheets.

Allie lay there and thought about what had transpired the night before. Did she and Zak really make mad passionate love? She was in a state of nirvana mingled with a bit of shock. It had been an incredible experience that Allie will never forget. But what now, how did they go forward from here? Would they still remain best friends?

Before Allie had too much time to contemplate those questions, Zak started to wake up. Allie leaned into him on one elbow and planted a tender kiss on his full, sexy mouth.

He opened his chocolate brown eyes and said to her "Good morning, beautiful." "Good morning babydoll," Allie replied.

Zak kind of giggled under his breath and smiled. "I think the name suits you perfectly after last night," said Allie.

"Whatever my princess wants to call me is just perfect," Zak said. "You know Allie, I have been in love with you since we met. I don't know why I have waited so long to tell you."

"Oh Zak, I have been head over heels in love with you, too." Zak pulled her close to him, and they embraced and kissed passionately once again.

Allie climbed on top of Zak and made love to him slow and easy. Zak fondled her soft and full breasts, and she rode him until she reached a creamy orgasm that dripped down to his massive balls. As soon as he felt her pussy cream reach his balls, they drew up, and he shot a full load of spunk deep inside Allie.

He and Allie both groaned in harmonious ecstasy as they came into each other's arms. Allie was so erotic and excited that she came three more times. Zak couldn't stop her from coming all over him and he loved it. His little bookworm had become a wild animal in bed!

The third time Allie came Zak took notice of every detail. He noticed the sexy "come hither" expression on her freckled face, the way she arched her back ever so slightly and the way her strawberry blonde locks turned into a massive tousle of sexy curls. Zak had always been turned on by women who squirted their pussies, and Allie seemed to have that talent and then some. Allie truly was his dream woman.

When Allie finally collapsed into a beautiful clump on the bed beside him, Zak said, "You are perfect princess and I adore you."

"I adore you too babydoll. I sure did wet down the sheets didn't I?" Allie giggled. "Yes you did and I loved it, you naughty girl. You are so fucking hot!" replied Zak. Allie jumped up from the bed naked and ran playfully to the shower with Zak hot on her sexy trail. Once in the shower, she stroked Zak's cock to another huge erection.

She could tell he wanted to squirt all over her face. Allie kneeled down with the water trickling down her face and sucked the fuck out of his delicious dick. She playfully circled the head and rim and drove him wild with anticipation. By the time she swallowed his luscious cock down to his enormous balls, he unloaded deep in her throat. Just as the last load was about to spurt from the end, Allie yanked it out of her mouth and jacked it to its last release of hot sweet cum.

Allie then looked up at Zak and sexily licked the love seed from the corners of her mouth, and then said, "I hope you liked that babydoll!" She shook her tight little ass at him, hopped from the shower and went downstairs to make Zak's second breakfast.

The next couple of days were incredible between Zak and Allie. They went to the beach in Corpus Christie and made love by the incoming waves just like in the movies. They built a fire by the ocean and held each other tight beneath a blanket and watched the sunrise together. Allie was so in love with Zak it made her frightened. She knew if she ever lost him she couldn't stand it. "Zak, what will happen if our love doesn't survive?" Allie asked.

"Allie, I wish you would quit doubting us and let us just be in love." But Allie was filled with insecurities that she could not contain or handle.

Suddenly, Allie jumped up from the blanket and wanted to go back to Houston. She suddenly became angry and said some regretful words to hurt Zak. Allie really didn't know why she was doing it.

The words just flew from her mouth: "You are nothing but a playboy, Zak. You will hurt me probably worse than Justin." "Allie I will not. Why are you saying these things to me?"

"I don't know Zak. Let's just go back to the city NOW!" Allie threw her bag in the back seat and slumped down in the passenger's side and didn't say a word to Zak the whole ride back.

Zak couldn't understand why Allie had become so upset with him. He had no intention of breaking her heart like those other jerks, but Allie didn't realize that. She was consumed with the pain of her past relationships. She was letting jealousy eat her up inside. They haunted her and tormented her.

Allie went inside her house and back to her bedroom and had a good cry. About an hour later, Zak came in and sat down beside her and stroked her hair.

"What's up princess? Why did you get so upset?" Zak asked.

"I don't really know Zak, but I am just having some trust issues right now. When

Justin deceived me, I was devastated Zak. Do you know what it feels like for someone to proclaim undying love to you and then in one minute's notice you find out everything that you had believed in was a complete lie?" "I'm sure it hurts Allie, but not all men are like that." "Maybe not Zak, but just think, what if the girl you thought the world of doesn't only say you were her whole life but constantly tells you she could never hurt you and that it would kill her to lose you, yet you found out that what she meant is the opposite? What if you found out she intentionally played you for a fool?"

Allie started to cry again, and Zak consoled her in his ample arms. But before either of them could control themselves, they were ravaging one another's bodies again. The soft kisses turned to hungry and starving ones. Zak lifted up Allie's hair and kissed her delicious neck all over, sending goose bumps of electrical pulses racing from the top of her red hair to her toes and back up again. Her neck tasted of maple and honey, thought Zak, two of his favorite flavors in the world. "Talk dirty to me baby. Tell me how fucking hot I am" said Allie.

"You are the most delicious woman I have ever tasted, and I could get intoxicated on your fumes," replied Zak who now had a pretty substantial boner growing in his warm ups.

"Do you want to eat my pussy and drink my sweet cream baby?" said Allie in an ultra-naughty voice that made Zak leak spunk from his swelling dick head.

"Fuck!" said Zak. "Hell yes! I want to eat that drenched snatch right now. I want to bury my face in your crotch and slurp every drop of your pussy cum. Allie groped for his 8-inch cock and held it firmly in her hands and teased him.

"Is this cock hurting? Do you want it fucked and sucked right now?"

"Mmmmm," Zak groaned in the sexiest animal-like expression of lust Allie had ever heard. She ever so slightly put a few of her fingers inside his warm ups and stroked the rim around the head of Zak's cock until he jerked with pre-orgasmic jolts throughout his hot body.

Allie noticed the amazing look that came across Zak's face when he was hot and horny like he was right then. It made her pussy leak a stream of squirt down her legs. "Eat my wet and horny pussy right now," groaned Allie.

Zak laid Allie back onto the bed and slowly licked the inside of her milky white thighs. This action alone made Allie do that sexy back arch and throw her head back that made Zak nearly cum right then and there. Allie guided Zak's head with her hands.

"Pull my meaty lips with your mouth. Eat that pussy up baby!" Zak groaned and slurped the cream that was now oozing from Allie's hot snatch. "Fuck!" thought Zak, this is the sweetest fucking red hot pussy I have ever had in my mouth." He pulled her lips one at a time and discovered that her left one was most sensitive. He sucked it by itself and Allie started to orgasm.

Zak could hardly contain the spasms in her

enraptured body. She arched high off the bed and squirted a stream of pussy cum that wet Zak down all over his face. It was the hottest moment of Zak's life. Once she started the second orgasm, Zak couldn't stop his hard boner. He came all over himself at the same time he drank of the sweetest nectar he had ever tasted.

After Zak was able to pry his face away from Allie's hot bits and come up for air, he said to her, "Why don't you sit down on top of my dick and ride me reverse cowgirl style?"

"Okay baby, do you want me to ride you slow and hot? Or do you want me to bounce up and down like a rodeo clown on that big member?" Allie asked playfully.

"How about you ride me any way that you want princess," Zak said as he reached in to kiss Allie lovingly.

Allie mounted Zak reverse cowgirl style and decided she preferred to ride him slow and seductive. This way, she could feel every inch of him as he slid in and out of her. Zak watched Allie's gorgeous back as she rode him like a horny cowgirl. "Yee haw! Babydoll!" said Zak as Allie plunged up and down on his soaking wet cock.

Zak could tell that Allie was nearing her orgasm because her ripe lush lips gripped his cock like there was no tomorrow. Her pussy had a hold of his cock that wasn't going to let up until she gushed her juice all over his lap.

"Baby, Babyyyyyyy..." Allie screamed. "I am about to cum on you!" About that time, Zak felt a surge of hot, creamy orgasmic liquid flow down his dick and his lap and ultimately down his upper thighs. Allie was in a state of pure paradise with her back arched head back and red hair flying.

One sight of this gorgeous passionate woman covering him in juice caused Zak to start shooting his load way deep inside Allie's hot love box. Zak started with a low bear rumble at the beginning of his orgasm until he ended in full blown groans that shook the foundations of the house it seemed. This was the single most sexually intense moment of his life thought Zak, but he had a feeling with Allie Sommers at the helm there would be many more moments like this to come.

When the two of them finally came back to reality from the trip to Venus they just took, they looked at each other and chuckled and kissed and acted like two little kids. "I am so in love with you Allie," said Zak.

"I am way more in love with you baby doll," said Allie.

"No way!" replied Zak. "Yes, way," giggled Allie. The two of them fell asleep that night intertwined together like two pieces of twine. This was a love that nothing could stop. It had the driving passion of a freight train and the fire of a volcano.

(4 Months Later)

The last four months had been a challenge for Zak and Allie for sure. They had braved some pretty tumultuous storms in their relationship. Allie had to deal with her personal struggle with trust and jealousy. It was very difficult for her at first. A raving beauty named Kimberly had shown up on their doorstep one day sending Allie into a fire-breathing fit of passionate jealousy. She was Zak's ex, and sure she was hot as fuck, but Zak didn't want her. Whether Allie believed it or not, Zak was crazy about her. He actually moved out for a week in the heart of the turmoil, but he couldn't stay away from his princess Allie.

He adored every single delicious, infuriating, annoying, adorable, sexy, mischievous thing about her. He contemplated ending it all over her jealousy, but he could not live without the passion of her in his life. One thing about Allie Sommers is that she loved Zak Freemont like crazy, and she always would.

Allie had agreed to get counseling for her jealousy, and Zak felt it was helping her. Today was a big day for Zak and Allie; they were embarking on a new adventure together. Allie was so excited. In fact, Zak was just about to call her cell phone and see what was taking her so long when he saw Allie's car coming down the street. .Zak went out to the driveway to meet Allie, and she leapt into his arms, "Oh Zak, I am so excited! Can you believe we are actually moving to New York City in the morning?"

Zak and Allie had made some major changes in their lives over the past few months. Zak had taken a job as a Marine recruiter in a prestigious New York recruiting office, and Allie would be working with underprivileged children in the inner city. It would be a whole new lifestyle for them, but they were incredibly excited about it. "I am so in love with you princess, and I always will be. You believe me right?"

"Yes babydoll, I believe you and I am way more in love with you by the way," replied Allie.

"Come here, you hot woman, and give your man a kiss!" said Zak.

Allie flashed her sparkling smile and looked up at Zak with that familiar twinkle in her eyes and said, "Catch me if you can!" Allie took off running in the house and Zak followed right behind her hot on her sexy trail as always. They made mad passionate love and collapsed in each other's arms, both dreaming of the new life they had for them just waiting around the corner.

6 FAITH RETURNS

Preface

Faith Latimer couldn't believe what she was hearing her brother say on the phone. "Billy, please slow down. Billy, I don't understand what you are trying to say," Faith said.

"It's Dad, Faith. He is very sick and probably only has days left to live. The doctors have found an aneurysm that can kill him instantly. You need to get home, now," Faith's brother, Billy said.

Faith sat in the window seat of the Continental jet headed to Cheyenne Wyoming. Faith had grown up in the beautiful state, on a ranch, in a smaller town in Wyoming, known as Cedarfalls. Her dad was a rancher, and had been, since he was a teenager himself. Her mom took care of Faith and her little brother, Billy. She cooked, canned vegetables, gardened, and sewed. She did all of the things that Faith never did now.

Faith had decided to leave Wyoming just out of high school and follow a big time designing career. She got accepted into a prestigious school of design, in New York City, and moved away from home only a few months after graduating.

Faith's mom had died of cancer when she was only 15 years old. So Faith had to, basically, be the mom and the cook.

After a few years of that, she learned to resent her dad and this made her want to leave Wyoming after high school, even more than ever. She missed out on her youth and didn't get to do things like other kids she knew. Also, she grew up on a rural ranch, which Faith didn't care for much, either. Wyoming didn't have enough to spark Faith's interest. She had plans of going to design school in New York City, right after high school.

Now look at her. She was gorgeous, with a chestnut, collarbone length, bob haircut with loads of waves and curls, bright blue eyes, and long legs that always got the men's attention.

Faith was 5'7", without heels, and had a beautiful statuesque presence. She could easily be mistaken for a fashion model. She had exotic good looks.

Faith was not looking forward to returning home to "The Painted Sky Ranch." She hadn't been home to the ranch in nearly 10 years. She was very anxious and uptight about the whole thing.

She had no idea how she would deal with her dad's impending death, or Billy's constant questions and guilt trips. She only had a few minutes until the plane landed. She was very nervous to see her brother, again.

As Faith walked off the ramp, into the airport, she looked around for Billy. She was just about to decide he wasn't there when she saw him. He gestured to her and she walked up to him.

"Hi, little brother, long time no see," Faith said. She and Billy embraced and it felt good hugging her brother. It had been a long time.

"Faith, you look terrific," Billy said. "It seems that city life is agreeing with you."

"Thank you little brother. I like the city life. It suits me pretty well" Faith said.

She and her brother talked all the way home, recounting memories and laughing at old stories.

Then, the conversation turned to their father, Pete Latimer, and his aneurism. "How bad off is he, Billy?" asked Faith.

"He's pretty darn bad, Faith. It looks like he is on his deathbed. The doctor allowed him to come home and be comfortable."

When Billy pulled the Chevy truck into Painted Sky Ranch, the scene was literally breathtaking. Faith had forgotten how exquisite the sunsets in Wyoming were. The mountains formed a purple haze across the sky.

Faith hadn't seen anything so beautiful in a

long time. She and Billy took Faith's bags inside and she headed upstairs to her old room with them. Her room really hadn't changed much. Her posters of Boys 2 Men were still on her wall, although they now looked faded. The pale pink bedspread was still on her fill sized bed and her pink walls had faded to a pale rose color.

Faith put her stuff away, then went downstairs to join her brother. She avoided her dad's room, at the far end of the hall. She wasn't quite sure what to say to him, yet.

"What are you making for supper little brother?" Faith asked.

"I thought I would fry us some chicken and I made some homemade potato salad earlier."

"That sounds delicious." Faith said.

After eating dinner, Faith and Billy went upstairs to visit their dad. When she first looked at him, Faith couldn't believe how sick and how pale her dad looked. She walked over to his bed and grabbed his hand. It was ice cold. Tears swelled up in Faith's eyes.

"He's had his meds tonight, Faith," Billy said. "Let's let him rest comfortably."

Faith and Billy left her dad's room. As Faith headed down the hall, to her room, she saw a man entering another bedroom. They caught a glimpse of each other and Faith swore she felt some sort of power, almost like a brush of the wind. That must be the rancher that Billy told her about, she thought. Faith was dead tired, so she crawled up under the covers and went right to sleep.

The next morning, very early, Faith was awakened by the sound of the rooster crowing his morning cock-a-doodle-doo. "What time is it, anyway?" Faith said with groggy eyes, rubbing them, trying to get awake. "What the fuck! It's only 5 am! What is wrong with these people?'" Faith mumbled.

She grabbed her white robe from the hook and went downstairs, rubbing her blue eyes. "Morning glory!" said an overly happy Billy.

"Yeah, yeah, where's the coffee?" Faith said, with closed eyes.

"Madame, at your service," said an unfamiliar voice.

Faith looked up with, finally, opened eyes, to a handsome and rugged man holding out a piping hot mug of coffee to her. "Thank you. I'm Faith Latimer, nice to meet you."

"The pleasure is all mine. I'm Luke Garrett and nice to meet you as well."

Faith kind of rustled her fingers through her hair, suddenly feeling about as attractive as a baboon's butt.

Luke was thinking to himself that this was the most beautiful woman he had ever laid eyes on. Even though her hair was a mess and she had no makeup on, there was something about this lady that set Luke's heart on fire. There was definitely something special about this lady, thought Luke, and he aimed to find out what, exactly, that was.

At the same time, Faith was feeling about

the same way for Luke. She looked him over and sized him up, as he ate his breakfast and chatted. He was handsome in a rugged and hard, working kind of way. He had manly, calloused hands and a strong jaw that really got Faith excited in more places than one. Billy had to get to work, in town. He was the local veterinarian and he had a very busy practice.

She knew that Luke had played a big role in taking care of her dad over these past few months and she was grateful for that. "Your dad is going downhill, more every day, and it is very upsetting for me. He gave me my first job on a ranch and I am very thankful to him for that," Luke said. Luke gathered her dad's medicine and some juice, and a bowl of oatmeal. Then, the two of them headed upstairs.

"Knock, knock, anybody awake?" Luke said, as he and Faith entered Pete's bedroom. "How are you feeling today?" Luke asked.

"I'm hanging in there," said Pete, in a weak voice.

"Hi Daddy, it's me, Faith," she said.

"Hi sweetheart, it's good to see you. You look beautiful," Pete said.

"I'm sorry to hear you are feeling so bad," Faith said. "We're here for you, dad. Now, you just rest and let us know if you need us."

Faith and Luke left her dad resting peacefully and walked out, into the hall. "Well, I better be getting to work and feeding the animals, and such," Luke said.

"Ok. I'll bring you some lemonade down later, if you like," Faith said.

"That would be great," Luke said, and he headed outside for a long morning at work.

Faith had been puttering around the house looking at old photos and things, and looked up at the clock to notice it was about 11 o'clock. Faith decided to make up a picnic basket, to take down to Luke. He had worked hard all morning. Faith figured it was the least she could do. Luke had done so much for her and her family. Faith packed some of the leftover chicken and potato salad. She packed up a few rolls, and some chocolate chip cookies for dessert. Earlier, she had made up a pitcher of lemonade. She brought that, along with some plastic cutlery and dishes, and headed outdoors.

Faith walked down, to where Luke was working hard repairing some pieces of wood in the stable. He looked up to see a beautiful vision before his eyes. Faith was standing there in a hot pink halter top and short blue jean cutoffs that showed off her long and sexy legs. "Hi there, are you hungry?" Faith said, toting her picnic basket.

"Yes, I am, as a matter of fact. Thank you for doing this, Faith," Luke said.

"No problem. We had plenty of fried chicken left, and potato salad, so I made us a picnic," Faith replied with flashing a huge smile at Luke.

They chose a huge shady tree to spread

their blanket under to eat their lunch. Faith couldn't help but notice the strong virile muscles that lie underneath Luke's work shirt. His hands were calloused and sexy. Luke was getting a hard on, just looking at Faith's gorgeous body sprawled out on the blanket. She was absolutely breathtaking in the noontime sun.

Faith and Luke discussed her life in Wyoming and her discontentment with her dad growing up. She felt that she had missed a lot of her childhood, having to take care of her brother and her dad.

As they talked, it was obvious there was a sexual tension in the air of Wyoming that could not be ignored. When Faith moved around a bit, on the blanket, Luke could see just a tiny bit of pussy hair out of the sides of her cutoffs. That really excited him and made his cock all the more uncomfortable, in his Levi's. Faith caught Luke looking at her snatch and she tried to open her legs, just a little farther, so as to give him a glimpse of possibly a lip. She was successful and that did it. Luke moved toward her, with his obvious hard dick in his pants.

He came towards Faith and the two of them engaged in a passionate kiss that was like nothing either of them had ever experienced.

"Should we do this?" Faith asked Luke.

"I noticed the nurse arrived when I was leaving" she said.

"It will be fine. She can't see us down here," Luke said who was now pulling Faith's pink shirt off of her, to reveal her gorgeous breasts.

Faith had nearly perfect tits, a sized 36-C.

Luke took her beautiful breasts and cupped them in his strong hands, but gently suckled them, until they came to pointed tips of sheer ecstasy. "Your tits are absolutely gorgeous," Luke said, as he now started to eat and lick them ravenously.

Faith was in complete erotic nirvana as Luke groped her body, licked her flesh, and plunged two of his calloused fingers deep inside her throbbing pussy.

"Fuck, you turn me on," Faith said, in a moaning and breathless voice.

"I love how wet you are getting for me," Luke said, in a gravelly voice that drove Faith to her knees. She seductively unzipped her shorts to reveal her pretty pussy, with a chestnut colored landing strip.

Luke fondled her very moist pussy, causing Faith to let out multiple moans of sheer ecstasy. Faith reached down and unzipped the bulging cock pressing hard against Luke's Levis. It popped out of his pants, hard as a rock and ready to pound her pussy hard and good. Faith lay down on the blanket and Luke mounted her on top. Then, slowly, but very proficiently, he pulled his steel hard dick in and out of her slippery snatch.

"Mmm... that feels divine," Faith said who could feel his peter rubbing against her g-spot.

"Your pussy is so sweet and so delicious." Luke said. "Do you mind if I go down on it, now?"

"After you let me lick my pussy juice off your cock you can," Faith said.

He rose up and put his cock right by her

mouth, and she hungrily ate her own pussy nectar off of his throbbing muscle. "Damn, I taste good and sweet," Faith said.

That comment drove Luke wild. He went down on her furry cunt and ate the fuck out of it. He moved his head back and forth, side to side, real fast. This action made Faith nearly cum right then and there. Then, he took his two fingers and spread her lips wide open. He lightly flicked on her bulbous clit with his tongue. Faith then began to hump his face and chin, furiously wanting to squirt all over his face.

Just then, he stopped eating her out and went up to kiss her. Faith ravenously ate her own pussy off of his face.

"Damn, I taste good. I could cum just tasting my hot snatch on your mouth. You are getting me so fucking horny," Faith said.

Luke and Faith kissed. Luke re-entered her seething hot pussy. Her hot lips ravenously gripped his cock and were so hungry for each other. He plunged his cock in, harder and harder, until he felt his balls draw up, ready to explode massive wads of cock cum inside Faith's starving pussy. They both rocked their bodies together in lascivious waves of passion, until suddenly, they both hit orgasm's peak at full capacity.

After making love in the noonday sun, Luke and Faith ran to the pond and skinny dipped for about 30 minutes.

"I'm not usually this bold with a man," Faith said. "There is just something about you, Luke Garrett, that intrigues me."

"You are very captivating to me as well. Are

you happy to be home in Wyoming, at all? Or, is your heart in the city?" Luke asked lovingly.

"I'm not really sure. I was anxious to leave here as a teenager, basically, but I must admit, now that I am 10 years older, it does seem rather serene and relaxing," Faith said.

Suddenly, she took off swimming across the pond, daring Luke to catch her. He finally caught her and they kissed passionately in the water. Luke fingered Faith under the water, bringing her to, yet, another mind-blowing orgasm that left her breathless.

They got out of the water and got dressed. Then, Luke offered to walk her back up to the house. When they got up to the house, they met the nurse at the door.

"How is my dad doing?" Faith asked.

"He's hanging in there," said the nurse. "But, it still doesn't look very hopeful. The doctors increased his meds, so maybe, he can rest more comfortably now." The nurse said and Luke gave Faith a warm embrace and told her she should call Billy, and let him know.

Billy came to the house after work, to see how his sister and dad were doing. "I don't know Billy. I think he has taken a turn for the worse," Faith said.

The two of them headed upstairs to see her dad. He was barely able to speak and was going in and out of consciousness. Faith tried to adjust his pillow and cool his head with a cloth. She tried everything she could to ease his pain. She had to admit it was getting to her, seeing her dad suffering like this. She looked at Luke and nearly started to cry.

"Come on Faith. Why don't we go for a stroll outside and get some fresh air?" Luke said, lovingly.

"Okay," Faith said, and they headed outside hand in hand. Billy had already left for the evening. It was only Faith and Luke at the house, besides her dying father.

Faith was starting to get a bit chilly in the night air. Also, a bit emotionally upset. She and Luke walked back in the house and heated up a little bit of soup that was frozen in containers, in the freezer. Faith went up to check on her dad, but he didn't look well at all. She went back downstairs in tears, not knowing exactly how to handle this kind of pain. Luke was waiting at the foot of the stairs and Faith just lunged into his arms, crying. He held her face in his hands and tried to tell her the most comforting words he could think of.

"Your dad would want you to be strong Faith. He wouldn't want you to cry," Luke said.

"I know. It is just that I have so many regrets," Faith said. Luke led her upstairs, to her room.

Once behind closed doors, Faith and Luke could not resist the urge to kiss passionately and erotically. Before long, their kisses turned into ravenous hands all over each other's body. Faith needed comfort and Luke was just the man to provide it to her.

They made their way over to the bed and Faith said to Luke, "Why don't you lie back and let me suck that big cock of yours?"

"That sounds wonderful," Luke said, sexily. So, he lay back, like Faith said, and let her go to work on his throbbing muscle.

"Damn, baby you suck my cock like you know exactly what you are doing." Luke said, very amorously. He could hear the whistling of the wind and the chimes outside, as Faith sucked harder and deeper, damn near to his balls. She went up and down on the shaft, circling her tongue around the red, hot tip of his head, driving him half wild with wanton pleasure. She looked up at him, with bold seductive eyes, driving him even closer to orgasm's release. Luke absolutely loved the look of passion and pleasure in Faith's beautiful steel blue eyes.

Faith sucked him very hard, right up until the point where he was about to shoot his seed down her throat, and she let off of his dick with a big suction that drove him insane with desire.

Then, Faith got on all fours on the bed and said, "Bang me baby, doggie style. I want you to see that bulging dick sliding in and out of me."

Luke entered her slick pussy from behind and began to grind in and out of her, painfully slow. With each pull and thrust, his cock head rubbed the tender g-spot inside Faith, giving her waves of molten pleasure.

As their bodies moved in intricate and beautiful rhythms, it seemed as if their seething flesh spilled love juices upon the bed.

They both came to a surreal orgasm, at precisely the same time, and groaned loudly, like sex hungry animals. In the other room, Faith's dad did not budge, nor did he ever hear a thing.

The next morning, Faith woke up in the arms of Luke Garrett. He was absolutely amazing. Faith felt as though she was on a roller coaster with all kinds of bends and turns. She felt as though she was in love for the very first time. She decided to get up and go check on her dad early this morning, before waking Luke up. She lightly knocked on her dad's bedroom door. She started to walk in and didn't see anything in particular, but she felt that something was different somehow.

She walked across the room, over to her dad's bed, and picked up his hand to give him a squeeze. She immediately noticed it! His hand was ice cold, thought Faith.

"Oh my God! Dad, are you okay?" Faith said, as she touched his face and felt for the pulse in his neck. She was quite certain her dad had passed away.

Immediately, a flood of tears came flowing like rivers down her face. She, then, began to wish she had spent more time with her dad over these past years. The guilt she felt inside could hardly be contained. Faith rushed back to her bedroom and woke up Luke.

"Luke, my dad is gone. He has passed away," Faith said through a flood of tears.

"Come here darling," Luke said, and he soothed her for a bit. "We better call Billy right away," Luke said.

Luke handled the phone calls, while Faith

took a shower and grieved the loss of her dad.

The next few days were very busy ones for Luke, Billy, and Faith. They had to make the appropriate funeral arrangements and call family members. They also had to prepare some delicious foods and have some catered, for the family to come over after the funeral. On the night before the funeral, Pete's lawyer was due to show up around 7 to read Pete's will to Billy and Faith. The lawyer arrived right on time, with all of the necessary papers.

He read through several odds and ends on the will. Pete left a fair amount of money, in appreciation, to Luke. Luke was grateful, of course, but he would have loved to stay on at the ranch, as opposed to selling it. Finally, the lawyer reached the part of the will that told who Mr. Latimer had left his ranch to. To everyone's surprise, he left every acre of it, and everything on it, to Faith.

Faith nearly fainted on the spot. "This must be some sort of mistake," Faith said.

"No, Miss Latimer, your father was quite clear," the attorney said.

Faith looked at Billy and Luke confused and really upset. "I have no idea what to do, now. I live in New York. I can't run a ranch," Faith said. Faith needed some time to be alone. So, she went upstairs on her bed and cried herself to sleep, just like she used to do.

After helping Billy clean up the supper

dishes, and seeing him and the attorney out, Luke headed upstairs to see if he could do anything to comfort Faith. He was very worried about her. She was so upset this afternoon and evening. "Knock knock..." Luke said, as he knocked lightly on Faith's bedroom door.

The knocking roused Faith from her half-asleep state. "Come on in," hollered Faith. "Hey baby, how are you doing?" Luke said, tenderly.

"I'm just torn, Luke. On the one hand, I have a very nice life and good job, back in New York, but on the other hand I know how much this ranch meant to my dad," Faith said, in a distraught sounding voice. "I would probably sell the ranch, if it was totally up to me and my wishes, but it isn't!"

She slumped into Luke's broad chest and cried. Soon, her tears turned to kisses to Luke's greedy mouth.

The desire between them grew stronger and more passionate. Luke was certainly growing on Faith, in many ways. His cock was growing, too, and he used it to jack her clit a little bit, before he put Faith's long, luscious, legs behind her ears and pumped her hard. He looked Faith right in the eyes while he plunged harder, deeper, and faster. He knew he was just about to unload a huge wad of hot spunk inside her hairy snatch. He started to growl and moan a huge moan that made Faith's pussy spasm and grab him with her snapper, even harder than ever before. Her lips wrapped so tight around his cock, he about had a nut over and over again.

"Damn, your pussy is hot baby," he said to Faith. "It is the sweetest, wettest, and hottest cunt I have ever fucked." Luke was still jerking a bit, from the amazing spunk load he just put inside Faith's horny as fuck pussy.

Faith then, suddenly, went down on his peter with an eager mouth, to eat her juices. "I am a nasty girl. I love my own pussy cum. If I could, I'd eat myself off for you baby. I'd love to squirt my own face down," she said. "Fuck that is hot as hell." As she was eating her pussy cream off his dick, Luke came, again. He couldn't help it. This woman turned him the fuck on.

"Fuck my ass now, baby," Faith said. "No one knows this about me, but I am a nymphomaniac. I have to cum everyday, one way or the other. I've been masturbating since I was 13. I squirted my first squirt when I was 14. I damn near ate myself off, then," she said. "My tongue was so close to my clit I could taste it."

Her words were so fucking hot that Luke plunged inside her asshole, hard and fast, and they both creamed, again, together. Afterwards, Faith lay there, flicking her clit to a point on the tip, and making her pussy come to a screaming orgasm. She writhed and jerked on the bed, with the best clitoral squirt she had ever had. She kept squirting and Faith kept jerking. Her beautiful legs were drawn up by her ears exposing her big pink, meaty lips.

Finally, Faith came out of her orgasmic state of nirvana. For an hour or so, Luke held Faith tight in his arms and comforted her tears away. She and Luke both knew that she had a hard decision ahead of her. Should she sell the family ranch and say goodbye to Wyoming forever? Or, should Faith return?

The next four days were very busy and hectic. They buried their father, entertained old family and friends, and Faith thought about the hard choices before her. Finally, after all of the arrangements and burial were taken care of, and the last cousin had gone home, Faith knew it was time to tell Billy and Luke her decision.

She first talked privately with Billy. Then, she and Luke took a walk out, to the pond, where they first made passionate love. She embraced Luke and they kissed for several minutes.

Then, Faith looked up at Luke with sadness in her eyes. "Luke, I've decided to sell the ranch and go back to New York, to my friends and my job."

Luke felt as though he had been punched in the stomach. He grabbed Faith and did not want to let her go. "I am in love with you, Faith," Luke said.

"I know, me too. Now, I better go before it gets too late." Faith said. She ran as fast as she could, never looking back. She took her belongings and loaded them into the old Chevy truck her dad had left her as well.

She didn't want to see Luke again, until she

was out of there. She was tough. She could do this. She started down the highway and tears poured from Faith's eyes. Back at the ranch, Luke had to keep tears back as well. Faith was distraught with emotion and longing.

That evening, about sunset, Luke was doing the final chores around the ranch and making sure all was safe and secure, before turning in by him. God, he missed Faith. Just then, Luke heard a vehicle coming down the dirt path that led up to Painted Sky Ranch. It must be a family member that forgot something when they were here, thought Luke.

Luke took a closer look. He swore it looked like Faith's truck. By golly, it was Faith! Luke went running towards the truck. Faith threw it into park and ran straight into Luke's arms. "Baby, I love you. I cannot leave you," Faith said.

"Baby, I love you, too," replied Luke. "I just don't know how I could have lived without you, Faith."

"Now, you don't have to find out. I'm all yours, Luke," Faith said.

"That is music to my ears!" Luke replied. He picked Faith up and twirled her around a few times. Then, they kissed, right there in the purple sunset, knowing they would be in love forever and this ranch would be their home for years to come.

7 CLANDESTINE AFFAIR

Preface

Amber stood speechless and in shock reading the letter that her boyfriend Jonathon had apparently slipped under the door early that morning. Amber couldn't believe what she was reading. She and Jonathon were supposed to get married in two days, but this letter was a dear Jane letter. Jonathon was calling off their marriage and only two days before the ceremony. Amber was absolutely devastated and didn't know where to turn. The tears flooded her eyes and there was a pit in her stomach and it seemed the whole room went pitch black.

After the shock of her breakup just a little over a week ago, Amber couldn't believe she was on a plane headed for Las Vegas. She and Jonathon had planned to go there for their honeymoon among other places as well.

Amber had used mostly her money to buy the trip so she figured she may as well not waste it. Now as she was headed on a plane alone she was kind of regretting it. She had invited her best friend Nikki to come along but she couldn't get away from work. So here was 25 year old Amber Cole alone going to Las Vegas. What was she thinking?

She was thinking she was going to try and live it up, get drunk, party and gamble and get Jonathon out of her heart and her mind for good. Amber just hoped she wasn't kidding herself.

About an hour and a half later Amber was unlocking the door to her honeymoon suite. It made her very sad and nostalgic to come inside. This is the room she and Jonathon had picked out from the brochure. Damn him! How could he do this to her? Amber went inside the pale blue decorated honeymoon suite. There were white roses in vases, silk sheets on the bed and his and her towels hanging from the bars in the bathroom.

Amber decided she was not going to sit around feeling sorry for herself, so she decided to get showered and go downstairs and have some fun. She put on a tight little red dress and black high heels. She was looking hot tonight with her long blonde hair pulled up in a sexy French knot. Amber was one of those girls with a perfect body. She didn't act like she had it either and that was what made Amber so gorgeous. She was, but was nice to most everyone and she didn't have an egotistical attitude.

Once Amber got downstairs she was seated at a table by herself in the corner. She didn't want to seem too obvious that she was alone or lonely. The waiter came over and took amber's order. She ordered the Chef Salad and a Margarita on the rocks. Amber loved Margaritas more than any mixed drink.

Amber ate her salad and drank two mixed drinks. She was feeling a little light headed by now and decided to saunter over to the slot machines.

As she was playing the slots Amber could feel eyes on her. She looked up and there was a handsome Hispanic man staring at her. He flashed a grin that would melt a girl like butter. Damn he is hot, thought Amber. She had never even been with a Hispanic or foreign man before. This was very intriguing to her. She decided not to seem too eager so she went over to the Blackjack tables for a while and as she was sitting there a waiter came over and said, "the gentleman ordered this for you." She looked up and there he was again. He waved and smiled even bigger at her this time. He thought Amber was stunning and so sexy.

Amber decided just to head outside for some air. This was just getting weird, she thought. Amber sat outside on the deck for a while enjoying the night air and the stars.

While she was sitting there relaxing and taking in the atmosphere she heard a voice behind her. "You look exquisite this evening I must say."

Amber turned around like she knew he must be talking to someone else. "Are you talking to me?" said Amber.

"Yes I am," said the man.

"You don't even know me," said Amber. She noticed it was the same Hispanic man that bought her the drink inside. "We can change that you know," said the man with a look of lust in his eyes.

"Are you serious?" giggled Amber. He was taken aback. No woman had ever laughed at Matias Romero before. Who did she think she was?

"My name is Matias Romero," he said. "What is your name, beautiful lady?"

Amber actually felt herself blush and said "My name is Amber Cole. Nice to meet you Mr. Romero."

"Call me Matias please," he said.

"Ok Matias," said Amber.

"So what brings you to our casino?" he asked Amber with wanton eyes.

"It is kind of embarrassing and I really don't want to say," said Amber.

"It cannot be that bad," said Matias.

"Yes it is. It is worse!" said Amber. "I was jilted by my fiancée two days before we got married," Amber said turning red in the face.

"How could someone do that to such a stunning young woman as you?" asked Matias while at the same time melting Amber's heart.

Matias reached over and took Amber's face in his hands and then gave her a simple kiss on the cheek. Then he turned around and grabbed a beautiful hibiscus bloom and then came and put it behind Amber's ear. "This flower is lovely but not half as lovely as you," Matias said.

Amber looked up at him with her pretty brown eyes and said "That is so sweet, thank you," she said. Amber had a heartwarming personality that grew on everybody. She was a kindergarten teacher by profession and very good with kids as well.

"How about I walk you to your suite?" asked Matias.

"Okay, that will be nice." Amber replied.

Once upstairs she and Matias made small talk and he told her how he and his family owned the particular hotel and casino she was staying in.

"This is my suite," said Amber pointing in that direction. Matias opened the door and led her inside. "You are welcome to stay for a nightcap."

She was very surprised she said that. But she felt a comfort with Matias that was beyond explanation.

Matias said "Allow me to fix us a night cap. Any preferences?" he said.

"Surprise me," said Amber.

Matias poured couple of brandies and brought Amber her glass. He sat down beside her on the blue cushioned loveseat that was adorned with fluffy pillows and very cozy. He handed Amber her glass and she said, "Thank you. You are a true gentleman Matias."

Matias loved her saying that. Things of tradition meant more to him that he let on. As they drank their brandies and started to loosen up Matias noticed how stunning Amber truly was. He was used to dating women of his ethnicity. Amber was a refreshing change. Of course, his ex-wife Carmen would have a fit. Hopefully, she didn't find out.

Amber had lovely long tanned legs and golden skin with natural blonde wavy hair and big beautiful brown puppy dog eyes. Those eyes are what got to Matias. She could look at him with those eyes and probably get whatever she desired from him. Amber looked up at him and had a wanton look in her eyes that Matias could not resist.

Before they knew what hit them they were embraced in a hot and romantic kiss. There was a natural connection between them that they couldn't resist. The kisses were tasty and tantalizing. Matias had the yummiest mouth that Amber had ever tasted. He did tongue wars inside their mouth and moaned very sexily letting Amber know he wanted her NOW.

They stood up and hungrily started grabbing at each other's clothes trying to get them off. Once Matias had Amber's top part of her red dress down he started gently licking and sucking her big beautiful nipples on her 36D size tits. She had some beautiful tits and they tasted so sweet. "Your tits are so hot Amber," he said in that sultry Spanish accent of his. "They taste like honey they are so fucking sweet."

He started ravaging them trying to get them

both in his mouth at the same time. Amber started to feel amazingly warm and wet all over her dew drenched body. She was in need of some dick really bad. Matias then stared kissing down her neck to the back if her neck covering her in goose bumps all over her golden fleshed body. She lunged into his cock with her hips as if begging him to enter her at his own exotic risk.

While lavishing Matias with kisses that were on fire, Amber unzipped his trousers to reveal a large brown bulging member. This cock had a head on it that would hit her G-spot perfectly maybe even making her squirt a few cum wads for him and all over him. Amber didn't realize how fucking cock-starved she was until she started slamming her pussy all over Matias's Spanish meat.

Amber got up on all fours and stuck her sexy ass up in the air and also stuck her just as equally sexy slick pussy up there for Matias to delight himself in. Amber had just enough pussy hair to make it hot but enough shaved to make it modern and classy. She didn't usually do what she was doing right now with a man she just met but Matias was impossible to resist. Matias now entered her wet snatch from behind and began plowing like nobody's business.

"Damn baby, you got you some fine-ass pussy," said Matias looking down at his member sliding in and out of Amber's furry cunt. He could see Amber's swollen labia squeezing his cock head as it moved in and out of her. The slower the better because on the way out his cock head grazed her g-spot causing her the jerks and the quivers and it felt so damn hot, thought Amber.

They continued to move their bodies in hot motion as the passion played. After fucking Amber doggie style, Amber then told Matias to lie down and get ready for some real fun. Amber went down on Matias like he had never been sucked or blown before. She worked her way up and down the shaft paying close attention to the head and ridge. She flicked her tongue ever so lightly and gently around the head until Matias thought he'd shoot right off. But Amber let off when she saw his massive gonads draw up.

She had found that men love to be teased whether they admit it or not. When Matias had quit jerking his body, Amber suddenly went down with a full blown deep throat blitz. She buried Matias's cock deep inside her throat gagging from the girth of it. She had him submerged so deep in her throat that she could feel his brown balls on her chin. Just then Matias started to nut. His cock squirted hard and profusely drenching the back of Amber's throat where she had no choice but to swallow and she did. She swallowed every last drop of Matias's love juice.

Amber plopped down beside Matias and they looked each other straight in the eyes. Without saying a word they both knew there was a connection between them that would not easily be broken. They also both knew that hard choices and times may just be up ahead of them. They also both knew that somehow, believe it or not, they were falling in love.

Amber fell asleep in the arms of Matias Romero that night and slept more comfortably than she had in ages. She woke up a bit stunned to find herself closely entwined with a virtual stranger.

But he sure didn't feel like a stranger. He felt like the man of her wildest imagination and sweetest dreams. Amber looked at this gorgeous man while he slumbered. His skin was golden like the sun and his hair a silky jet black that looked almost blue. God he was a hunk!

Amber ever so lightly tried to sneak the softest of kisses onto Matias' rosy lips. But as soon as she did he engulfed her in a deep, wet passionate kiss that had her laying back down into his arms in no time at all. Matias once again made mad passionate love to Amber. He rode her long and slow until they both had mutual orgasms that practically made the earth move.

After they made love they took a shower together and had breakfast out on the deck of Amber's suite together.

"Well, I need to get to work," said Matias. "The casino doesn't run itself."

"What all do you do on your job?" asked Amber.

"A little bit of everything," said Matias very hurriedly. "Why don't you stop by the casino desk today and maybe we can have a nice lunch together. We will serve you the best steak and lobster in the house."

"Ok what time?" said Amber.

"Meet me at the front desk around 1." said Matias.

Around 1 pm Amber headed downstairs to the lobby of the hotel/casino. Amber looked around but didn't see anyone at the desk.

She walked a little past the desk and suddenly she overheard what sounded like a heated discussion coming from a small room. "Matias, I demand you give it to me or else!" said the woman.

"Carmen, be quiet. Somebody will hear you. I am giving all that the courts ordered me to and it is never enough for you!" replied Matias in a very aggravated tone of voice.

"I bet you wouldn't want your dirty little secret leaking to the press in Vegas now would you?" said the hateful woman.

"Carmen, I swear you keep your mouth shut about that or..." said Matias.

"...or you'll what Matias, huh?" the woman replied. "Are you threatening me Matias?" she said.

"No, but I want you to leave now. I am very busy." said Matias. Carmen stormed out of the office and flew past Amber at warped speed.

"Hello beautiful," said Matias to Amber who had a confused and questioning look on her face. "Never mind her. That is my ex-wife Carmen who is a greedy money grubber," said Matias.

"She seemed really upset over something," said Amber.

"Don't worry about it," said Matias. "She is just blowing off steam. Now what do you say we go get that delicious gourmet lunch I promised you," said Matias.

"Okay," said Amber suspiciously. "I'm ready whenever you are."

They went into a private room that more than likely was one of Matias' offices and sat down at a table set for two. There were candles lit all over and a bottle of champagne on ice just begging them to dive into.

"It looks lovely," said Amber as she said down at the table covered with a beautiful red cloth and white roses as a centerpiece.

Matias popped the cork on the champagne and poured them a glass. They both made a toast to a future filled with peace and happiness.

"Matias, what on earth was that woman talking about?" asked Amber.

"Look Amber, that was my ex who tried to find any way she can to drain me of money." said Matias. "A long time ago my family and I were involved in a few illegal affairs when it came to our money. But we are not like that now. I also have a little boy and I regularly pay his child support along with her alimony." Matias said in a tone that was becoming irritated.

The two of them finished their meal and Matias walked up behind Amber and pulled her close. He nuzzled the back of her neck underneath her beautiful long blonde hair. "You are stunningly exquisite, Amber," said Matias.

"Your fiancée's loss is my gain," said Matias who desperately wanted to make love to and screw Amber so bad his dick was protruding nearly out of his zipper.

"Your muscle is throbbing baby," said Amber in her best seductress tone. "I need you to fuck me with that big cock right now before I lose it with anticipation.

Without even removing all of their clothes or even lying down, Matias picked Amber up and stuck his cock in right under her skirt. He pulled her dress up to her hips and plowed her good. All the while she had her legs wrapped tight around his waist and he hoisted her up and down on his dick with a bouncing action that had them both soaring. Matias filled her with his girth and in this position he was hitting her horny g-spot every time he took a plunge deep inside.

"Fuck, baby that makes me almost squirt right here and now!" hollered Amber while she moaned out in ecstasy. "I want to do something. Lie down on the floor Matias."

She had special talents and she was about to show Matias a thing or two. Matias was on the floor and Amber hiked her dress up a bit further and then in a position that was hotter than fuck, she squatted right over Matias' face. Amber began to flick her clit furiously to make her pussy ultra horny. The faster she went the more it stood erect. Amber let her clit have it with all of the masturbation motion she could conjure up.

Suddenly, Amber's body grew rigid. She knew she was about to have an orgasm that would send her reeling. Suddenly Amber began to squirt off. Matias was in shock and in heaven. She started panting and moaning and her pussy let out about three more good squirts drenching Matias good.

"Damn, that was so hot," said Matias. He started jerking his cock profusely and his cock squirted dick cum all over Amber's tits and face. They both collapsed onto the floor in the stickiness of their lovemaking. They were out of breath but still horny and fervent and they both knew it wouldn't be much longer until they would be fucking like two animals again.

Amber decided to do a little sightseeing for the remainder of the afternoon. She had agreed to accompany Matias to the casino dance that night.

She went out for a bit of shopping and bought a gorgeous silver cocktail mini dress that complimented her sexy body to a "T." She had a pair of strappy silver numbers that would look perfect with it Amber thought. Amber showered, did her makeup and got all dolled up for the big party in the casino. After Amber felt like she looked suitable enough to go to the party she headed downstairs. Heads turned as Amber walked by. She truly was that beautiful!

Amber could not believe her eyes the casino looked more spectacular than ever before. There were tiny sparkling party lights strung everywhere that gave the whole casino a beautiful dazzle and arrangements of fresh flowers placed intricately truly gave the whole casino a beautiful ambience.

Matias rushed over to Amber and embraced her and said "Hello beautiful, you look good enough to eat!"

"There will be time for that later," said Amber in a sultry tone. Matias made the sound of a fake growl and flashed Amber a winning smile. Matias took Amber over to his family and did some quick introductions. It was easy to see that they were all sizing Amber up. They were interested to see what had won the heart of their son and brother over.

The casino was packed with people left and right. They were playing slots, drinking, eating, dancing and so much more. Matais asked Amber to have a dance with him. They danced cheek to cheek and also boogied 'til they just couldn't boogie no more. They were having one of the best nights and times of their lives. "Would you like a mixed drink?" Matais asked Amber.

"Sure," said Amber as she sat down at a table to wait for Matias.

Suddenly Carmen rushed over to the table and sat down angrily beside Amber.

"Hello," said Amber. "Can I help you with something?" Of course Amber knew it was Matias's ex-wife, Carmen.

"Do you know what you are getting involved in fucking around with my husband?" said Carmen hatefully.

"He is your ex-husband as I understand and no I don't know what you mean," said Amber.

"Matias has been involved in all sorts of illegal affairs. He is a criminal, blondie. If I were you I'd leave now and get away from him," said Carmen. "A criminal? In what way? I don't understand." replied Amber.

"Matias owes the government, loan sharks and God knows who else millions of dollars. He is not the gorgeous and heroic man you think he is," said Carmen. "He will eat you up and spit you out blondie. He'll cheat on you and lie to you and get you mixed up in all kinds of sordid affairs. If I were you I'd get on the first plane away from Matias Romero."

This is precisely what Amber did. Before Matias could even put two and two together, Amber was getting into a taxi headed for the nearest airport. There was no way she was getting hurt by another two timing lying son of a bitch! She was done with men thought Amber as the tears stung her eyes as the taxi flew down the interstate headed for the airport.

As Amber's plane took off she was very sad. As crazy as it sounded, she was beginning to have feelings for Matias. She thought maybe they were soul mates. They had an instant connection. She should have known he was going to screw her over. They were so opposite that they were unique and alike if that made any sense. Amber missed him already and she could faintly smell his cologne on her dress as she laid her head back and cried tears of regret over two lost loves.

Amber's plane landed that evening back home in Sante Fe, New Mexico. Needless to say Amber was not in the best of spirits. Just a few nights earlier, she was involved in the hottest fuck she had ever had. Now here she sat alone with a bag of Oreos in her lap swallowing and fighting back tears all at the same time.

Back in Las Vegas, Matias was asking all around if anyone had seen the beautiful blonde that he knew in his heart he was falling in love with. No one had seen Amber slip out into the night. Matias had been embroiled in a big scene with Carmen. She made a huge and embarrassing display in front of the whole casino. She had accused Matias of all sorts of wrong doings. She had made a huge public spectacle out of herself and Matias along with his whole family.

Most of Carmen's accusations had been false but a few of them had been true. Still Matias ran a smooth operation here and it most certainly dug into his business in a negative way. Finally, Matias got a lead on Amber. A cocktail waitress told Matias that she had seen a tall Spanish woman sitting at the table with the beautiful blonde he spoke of.

Damn it, thought Matias there was no telling what Carmen had told Amber. He knew that Amber was a good, law abiding citizen and that it wouldn't take much to upset her. He had to find Amber and tell her the truth. Matias started doing a bit of investigating to find out where he could find his beautiful angel Amber. It didn't take long before Matias had a pretty good idea where to find his beauty.

Matias rushed to the airport as fast as he could. There was no way that Amber Cole was slipping between his fingers. There was no way at all he was going to lose her. He knew that Amber was something special and he had to find her so he could tell her how much so. He had to tell Amber exactly how he felt.

Once Matias landed in Sante Fe he began rehearsing in his mind what he was going to say to Amber or better yet what he was going to do. He could not wait to look her in her deep brown eyes and plead for her love. Matias took a cab across town to the address he found through his searching for Amber. He was very nervous about it. He knew the cab was within five minutes of Amber's house. At least he hoped it was Amber's house.

The cab pulled up in the drive and Matias paid the cabby. He did ask the cabby to stay just in case he had the wrong address. Matias knew this was Amber's house before she even came to the door. He could just feel her presence there. Matias rang the doorbell and waited. Finally he hears footsteps coming across the wood floors inside the house. There is a huge lump in Matias' throat. Amber swung the door open and there was Matias much to her surprise. She started to shut the door in his face and Matias caught it before she could.

"Amber, please will you talk to me? I was worried about you," said Matias.

"Why were you worried? Didn't you have some money to steal or a crime to commit or something?" yelled Amber.

"Amber, that is ridiculous. I used to have a shady lifestyle but not anymore. I am falling in love with you Amber," said Matias in a seductive tone that Amber had a hard time refusing.

"You what?" said Amber through teary eyes.

"I said I was beginning to fall in love with you," said Matias and then taking Amber in his arms and kissing her with a wanton passion that only someone in passionate love could give to another.

Matias then yanked her shirt down off of her shoulders and began licking and kissing her gorgeous and moistened flesh with his full lips and hot tongue. He reached two fingers inside her shorts to feel a drenched, hot snatch at his fingertips. Her pussy sucked his fingers inside real tight causing Matias to gasp with horny desire. He could feel her pale peach lips writhing around his soaked fingers. He pulled his fingers out to reveal drenched fingers that he first fed to Amber. She loved tasting her own pussy and she moaned with pleasure as she swallowed her own cream down her throat.

"My pussy tastes very sweet... so much like nectar," Amber whispered in a sultry tone that damn near brought Matias to his knees. "I want you to lick and flick my cunt until I cream your face down."

Amber stayed put where she was standing there against the wall and Matias dropped to his knees and ate the fuck out of her right then and there. Amber lifted her foot to his shoulder and you could get a clear vision of her throbbing, smoldering pussy.

She humped his face with hip swerving motion that would cause any red blooded American man to shoot his load in his pants. In fact, Matias shot off once or twice in his pants but was waiting to fuck her brains out before releasing it all. Amber's body began to really rock and move at this point and she became weak in the knees from the ecstasy and the orgasm she knew she was right at the tip of. Matias at that point took the very end of his tongue and flicked her clit head fast and lightly barely grazing it and causing Amber to go into a ravenous horny fit.

Just then Amber grabbed his head with both of her hands and ground her wet pussy into his face as hard as she could possibly muster. Her pussy wasn't releasing Matias until it had its way with him. Her pussy was going to cream everywhere all over this irresistible man. Amber finally let go of the sweetest, nastiest and most intense orgasm she had ever had in her life. She jerked her body for what seemed like five solid minutes and then she came again this time squirting Matias down again.

Then Amber hopped to her knees and engulfed his bulging dick in her beautiful mouth. She deep throated down to his gigantic balls and looked up at this man with complete seduction in her eyes. The seductive power between Amber and Matias was literally oozing from walls and hanging in the air of this room they shared. They both knew they had a connection that nothing could bring down. It was written in the stars. Amber and Matias were to be together for as long as they both drew breath. After having the wildest and most exquisite oral sex either of them had ever had, they lay down on the floor and embraced and kissed for what seemed like a lifetime.

"Amber, I know this may seem out of line and kind of weird but I want to ask you something?" said Matias with a little boy grin on his face.

"What darling?" asked Amber.

"Will you make me the happiest man on earth and marry me, Amber?" asked Matias.

8 DESIRE WITHIN THE WORDS

5 Months Earlier

Carly was scanning the poetry site that she loved one morning trying to find some good poetry to read to help her relax. Poetry had a way of doing that for her. She went to scan the list of spotlighted poems and suddenly came upon the name of a poem that caught her eye. It was called "The Poet's Heart." Carly noticed it was written by a poet that called himself "Logbranch59."

Carly had tried to read his stuff before and found it incredibly complicated but still, she went for it because she liked the title.

As she read the piece, something in his smooth and mellow words got to Carly. He had such a way of weaving a rhyme. His words were like spun silk upon the page. Carly decided she had to see more about this man.

She went to his profile page to see the man behind these words. As odd as it sounds,

Carly had an instant connection with the picture of the man staring back at her. He wasn't your typical handsome good looks, but he was exactly what Carly found attractive in a man. He had a rugged yet dignified look about him that fascinated Carly. Carly also found him very sexy and hot.

As Carly scanned some of his beautiful poems, she felt as though she had known this man forever. As they often did on her poetry site, Carly reviewed some of his poetry. She went about her day doing the things she needed to get done and writing her articles as a freelance writer. As the evening approached, Carly needed to relax, so she logged onto her site. She immediately saw there was a private message for her from none other than Logbranch59. She opened her page and read his words in the message:

Hello my friend,

It was wonderful to get your message and review of my work. I am humbled by your kind words about my writings. I have in turn read some of yours, and you have a wonderful gift for the written word. I also couldn't help but notice that we live only four hours apart. I am your neighbor. I live in Missouri. I noticed your profile said you lived in Oklahoma. Also, may I be so bold as to ask for a snapshot of the person with whom I am speaking to? You've seen me. I'd love to put a face with your words. By the way, my name is Devon St. James. I hope to hear from you soon.

Carly was a bit mesmerized once again by Devon's sweet words and the apparent gift he had with words. Carly couldn't understand what on earth it was about Devon that got her excited, but it was definitely something. So before Carly knew it, she was sending him a head shot picture through the email.

Carly was quite ashamed that she had naughty thoughts at this time. She needed to snap out of this now! For a fleeting moment, she actually thought about removing her panties and showing him her meaty pussy. She had never done such a thing so soon with a man online, and she better not now, Carly thought.

"But it sure would be hot," she whispered underneath her breath.

Right at this time, Carly clicked send and off went her reply and head shot to this man she didn't know yet at all.

When Devon checked his mailbox on the poetry site, he was pleased to see a reply from that charming woman, Carly. He was excited to open it up, so he could see what Carly looked like. When he saw her, he was very pleased indeed. She had beautiful medium length auburn hair with a smile that lit up his world. She also had sparkling green eyes with a hint of impishness that drove him wild with desire. There was something about her that made her stand out from the countless others that Devon had courted with his words.

Devon admitted he had been a bit of a scoundrel in his day. He had spent 20 years in a loveless marriage, and since then, browsing the Internet for women to woo had become a lifestyle for the rogue.

In hindsight, Devon now wished he had listened to his intuition and never fell for Carly at all. He had a feeling that she would be the one to challenge him and shake up his world. If he only knew how true that was. After seeing her picture and thinking about the things she said, Devon wrote Carly another private message:

Hi Carly,

I just read your message and received your picture. You are beautiful! I love your hair. It is exactly what I love to see in a woman's hair, and I love green eyes too. It would be great to meet someday. Maybe the next time I travel for business, I can drop by and see you or we could do lunch somewhere, my treat of course. Holler back at me when you can. Your new friend, Devon.

Things progressed rather quickly for Carly and Devon. They chatted daily, read and reviewed each other's poetry and even chatted on the phone a few times. In fact, the night before Carly and Devon had some very hot phone sex that went on a few hours and ended up with them both having a mutual orgasm.

They both felt an instant connection like nothing else they had ever felt. Carly had enjoyed Devon's company over the last few months and found she was falling head over heels in love with him, or at least, crazy about him. Whether he wanted to admit it or not, Devon felt the very same way. Carly was gorgeous in his eyes, and she did things to him that no other woman could or ever would. Devon decided to call Carly on the phone and ask her if she was ready to take their affair to the next level.

The phone rang and Carly answered with a pleasant "Hello?"

"Hey beautiful, guess who?" said Devon.

Carly always buckled under the sound of his velvet voice.

"Hi, handsome man," replied Carly.

"So what's up? Miss me much?" asked Devon.

"I have missed you like crazy, that's all," said Carly.

"Well then, I was thinking maybe we could take our steamy romance up a notch. What do you say?" asked Devon.

"What did you have in mind?" said Carly sexily.

"Well I was thinking we could webcam. Maybe see each other's bodies up close and personal."

The thought of that drove Carly wild with anticipation.

"Okay. I have an article to finish, but I could get with you in about 30 minutes or so," said Carly.

"Okay sweetness, I'll see you then," said Devon and they hung up the phone.

Carly quickly put a few finishing touches on

her article and then fixed up a bit before seeing Devon live. She fixed her auburn hair in a sexy tousled style, freshened up her makeup, and put on a tight fitting little black dress with no panties.

That will drive him wild, thought Carly. Carly got situated in a comfortable chair with her laptop ready and her webcam ready to go. She was so excited she could hardly stand it, and just one thought of Devon got her vagina soaking wet with anticipation.

Just when Carly thought the anticipation would drive her insane, she heard a little alarm accompanied by a bell sound. Yes! It was her cyber lover coming to call. Carly clicked the bar and watched her screen anxiously waiting for the man she was nuts about to appear.

Suddenly, there he was waving and grinning at Carly seductively. Carly felt herself blush a bit, but she was still bold enough to flash him a bit of pussy as she crossed her legs and uncrossed them, very Sharon Stone in Basic Instinct.

"Damn," said Devon. "That was some hot shit baby!"

Carly giggled incessantly like some love struck teeny bopper. "Oh was it? How about this?" she said, as she plopped one of her big DD tits out for Devon to see.

Devon got bug-eyed and about fell out of his adjustable black computer chair. Suddenly, horny as fuck, Devon stood up and dropped his warm-ups to the floor revealing a very adorable half way hard cock. Carly named everything and of course she had names for their genitalia. She called her pussy Misty, because she liked to spray mist and Devon's dick Liam because it seemed Irish somehow to Carly. Some people would call Carly nuts, but Carly just thought she had a really active imagination.

"Put your fingers in that wet cunt and play with yourself, baby," said Devon whose eyes were getting darker green and bigger by the minute.

Carly, not being one to disagree, did as her lover asked and started to play with Misty.

"Mmm... it feels really wet and so fucking good baby," said Carly in a horny tone that Devon was beginning to recognize all too well.

She closed her eyes and threw her sexy head back to get the full pleasure of the finger fucking she was giving her hairy snatch. Devon was officially "boner-ized" by this time. He had pre-spunk flowing from his cock's eye even as she fingered her hole.

Carly opened her sparkling green peepers to catch a look at what her cyber cutie was doing to his adorable Liam. Devon was slowly and methodically jacking Liam to a boner of mass proportions Carly could see very well. Damn, he looked good, thought Carly as her fingers started to do double time inside her pussy hole.

"Put four fingers inside my pussy, baby," said Devon in a sexy voice that hinted of orgasm in the not so distant future.

Devon began stroking harder and longer strokes on his fat dick. Carly was slamming four fingers in and out of her cunt so fast her hands were nearly invisible. Devon could hear the soap dispenser-like wet hand every time Carly's fingers took the plunge. Devon knew orgasm-ville was right around the corner. Carly stared to moan in that gravely tone that Devon had fallen in love with.

She started to say, "Baby, Baby, Baby!!!" When Carly did that, she was on the heels of cumming and cumming good.

"Yes baby? Are you going to cum for me?" Devon asked.

"I am coming nowwwwww," Carly writhed and jerked and squirted all over her chair and damn near soaked her computer she lovingly named "Dell."

At this point, Devon was in full throttle wanking mode and started to squirt his thick penis everywhere. He first squirted one big wad of spunk and then three short but nonetheless hot spurts followed leaving Devon spent and breathless. "Damn, baby if we keep this up, I'm going to need an oxygen tank," said Devon.

Carly laughed on the other side of the cam and said, "Oh baby you are so fucking hot!" Knowing that this extremely virile man would be ready for round two as soon as you could say, "Jerk off with me baby!"

The days that followed turned out to be some of the most exciting days in either Carly or Devon's life. They were falling passionately in love, and there was nothing either of them could do to stop the freight drive driving force of emotions that overtook them. Carly had never had such strong desire or feelings for any man in her life, and it scared her to death! She knew that he held her heart in his hands. She also knew that if he ever hurt her, it might very well be the end for her.

She couldn't take it if that happened. She would try to explain to Devon these things, but he would always say, "Carly I will never hurt you. I couldn't. The thought of doing anything to hurt your tender heart would absolutely kill me."

After a bit of time, Carly started to believe all of the beautiful things that Devon said to her. He would tell her she was gorgeous and the most perfect woman for him. He would say she was his dream woman! Carly couldn't believe she had found such a perfect man who loves her.

On their poetry site, they kept their passionate love affair quiet. Carly posted poems that were about Devon but no one knew. She would mysteriously say they were to her "muse." Devon would then answer her poetry in return with loving words and desire within those words.

It was obvious these two people were madly in love and crazy about one another. The other poets on the site were ecstatic even though they weren't sure quite yet exactly who had stolen Carly's heart. Carly was a favorite on the site, and she had written over 500 pieces of poetry and prose. Carly was a good writer who put her heart into everything that she penned. As their love grew, Carly and Devon decided that they had to meet and consummate the feelings they had for one another.

Carly made the huge decision to uproot her life and move to Missouri to be with Devon. She knew she was taking a huge risk, but what if he was THE one? She decided that true love was worth it. So she headed to Missouri with love being the only thing on her mind.

When Carly drove up to the little duplex where Devon lived, she was incredibly nervous and excited all at the same time. Was she really doing this? She asked herself. Was she really risking everything for this man? Carly pulled up into the driveway anxious to get out of her vehicle. It had only been a 5-hour trip from Oklahoma to Missouri where Devon lived, but it had seemed like an eternity to Carly.

As Carly was heading up to the door, the door flung open suddenly, and it was Devon. Without even thinking about it, Carly ran and threw herself into his arms. They embraced and kissed right there on the porch nearly inseparable. Devon took her face into his hands and looked at her. "You are so beautiful," he said and then kissed her again madly and passionately.

"Come on in. I'll step out and get the rest of your things," said Devon. Together, they put Carly's things away in a few drawers that Devon had cleared out for her. They talk and reminisced like they had known each other a lifetime.

"Are you ready for dinner?" asked Devon.

Okay, what are we having?" asked Carly.

"I made a salad and rolls, and I thought we could grill some rib eyes," said Devon.

"Sounds delicious," said Carly.

The two of them had a nice dinner out on the deck and talked like old friends. It began to get chilly outside so the two of them headed back in the house. Carly sat down on the couch, and Devon turned on some soft music and lit a candle. He scooted in real close to Carly on the couch.

"I am so happy you came to stay with me for a while, Carly. I think that what we share is something rare and wonderful," said Devon.

"I do too, baby. I love you so much."

"I love you too, Carly. I have loved you practically since we first started chatting," replied Devon. The sparks between them began to heat up, and Devon and Carly could no longer contain the deep desire between them anymore.

Devon looked at Carly with love and lust written all over his face.

"Let's go to the bedroom. What do you say?" asked Devon.

Carly nodded, and they headed upstairs with her hand in Devon's. Once upstairs, Devon slowly began undressing Carly, all the while taking little breaks to kiss and nuzzle her neck.

"Your neck tastes incredible," said Devon.

"Mmm, it feels great when you kiss me that way," replied Carly in a breathy sultry tone.

Ravenously, Devon began to kiss her neck and touch Carly all over her excited body. He massaged her huge tits and kissed her hard pink nipples hungrily and greedily. The feel of his hands all over her body felt like little jolts of electricity to Carly. She could hardly contain her emotions and desire.

"Do you want me to suck your cock, baby?" whispered Carly into Devon's very eager ear.

"Sure, baby! Anything you want to do to me is just fine," replied Devon.

Carly dropped to her knees and slowly unzipped Devon's pants revealing his bulging member. As she was kneeling down in front of him, Devon looked down just in time to see a beautiful vision of her hairy pussy smiling at him. The lips were absolutely exquisite, thought Devon as his mouth watered just thinking about going down on it.

Carly took Devon's fat cock in her hands and stroked it ever so lightly. She took her fingertips and slowly stroked around the rim, driving Devon absolutely wild with desire.

"Fuck, that feels so hot!" said Devon.

Suddenly Carly took his throbbing dick in her mouth and started to suck vehemently. Devon was absolutely astounded at her expertise at sucking cock. No one had ever even come close to sucking it this good. Carly urged him to lay down on the bed, so she could do it even better.

"Does it feel good to have my mouth around Liam, baby?" asked Carly.

"It feels amazing. It's the best blowjob I have ever had," said Devon.

Carly smiled cheekily and continued on with her mission. What Devon loved so much about how Carly was sucking his cock is the fact that she did it like she wanted to do it and like she enjoyed it. In the past, Devon had never experienced a blowjob where the woman acted like she even wanted to do it. He could have easily shot in Carly's mouth in about five minutes of her superior sucking, but he didn't. Instead, Devon decided he wanted to make love to this very fascinating woman.

"Baby, why don't you lay back and allow me to make slow, sweet love to you?" said Devon. "I want you to experience what it is like to truly be made love to and not just fucked."

Carly laid back and let Devon take the reins. Devon mounted her in the missionary position and slowly pulled his rock hard cock in and out of her making Carly moan with unbelievable pleasure. The two of them made the best love that they had ever experienced. After they made love, the two of them lay in each other's arms for the entire night. Devon held Carly tight just like she liked. He thought to himself he would never in a million years let Carly go. He adored her so much.

For the next several weeks, the love between Carly and Devon grew and became more intense than either of them ever imagined it could be. Both of them wondered how they had ever managed to live without the other. They were ecstatically happy to say the least. They got along perfectly, in fact. It seemed as if they were like two peas in a pod. They finished each other's sentences, liked the same foods, watched the same movies, and loved the same literature. Everyone on their poetry site was so happy for Carly and Devon; it seemed as if they were a match made in heaven.

About four months after Carly moved in with Devon, she got some shocking news from back home. Carly's little sister Anna was in trouble.

Carly's mom called her one day very emotionally distraught. "Carly, we need you to come back to Oklahoma right away!" said her Mom over the phone.

"Why? What's wrong Mom?" Carly answered.

"It's Anna," cried her Mom. "She is in the mental hospital; she tried to kill herself, Carly!"

At that moment, Carly's heart dropped to the floor. Anna was her best friend in the whole world. Anna was the one regret Carly had. When she made the choice to move to Missouri to be with Devon, Anna had begged Carly to stay, but Carly was so intent on being with Devon she foolishly shrugged Anna off. She knew that Anna had been going through some rough times emotionally. She was a high school junior and a misfit. She had shown signs of being emotionally unstable about the time that Carly had met Devon.

Carly had tried to reach out to Anna, but Anna got worse and retreated into her shell. She had gotten in with the wrong crowd. She was into the dark things of life. Carly also suspected that Anna was a lesbian and into drugs. Pangs of guilt washed over Carly as her mother's voice kept talking over the phone.

"Carly, please come home as soon as possible. Anna says only you can make her feel better again."

"Let me see what I can do, Mom. Tell Anna I love her."

Carly hung up the phone and went upstairs threw herself on the bed crying tears of unbelievable pain.

About 30 minutes later, Devon got home from work and was looking for Carly. "Baby, where are you? You mean, I don't get greeted with a huge hug and a kiss today?" asked Devon.

He could hear Carly upstairs crying, so he raced up there to see what was wrong. "What's wrong, sweetness?" asked Devon tenderly.

Carly told Devon the whole sad story through tears and angst. Devon was stunned to say the least. He wished there was some way he could be of more help to Carly, but he was at a loss as to what to say or do. So all he could do was hold her while she cried tears of sadness.

Hugs of comfort slowly but surely turned to throws of passionate lovemaking between Devon and Carly. Devon loved Carly so much, and it killed him to see her so guilt ridden over her little sister Anna. In ways, Devon felt responsible. He felt as if it was his fault for pursuing Carly and ultimately talking her into moving to Missouri to join him. Deep in his heart, Devon knew that he was going to lose Carly, even if temporarily. He knew her. He knew that she had such a big heart that she would not be able to stay away from her sister if she needed her.

That night, Devon and Carly made love like it was the last time they would ever have the chance to. Devon wanted Carly to feel loved like she never had before.

He kissed her scrumptious neck slowly, and he made sure to give extra attention to that special place on her neck that she loved to be kissed and sucked so much. They kissed passionately playing tongue wars inside their mouths with their hungry tongues. Devon kissed and sucked both of Carly's huge pink nipples with his mouth, bringing her to moaning pleasure and making her arch her back begging for his cock to be put inside her wet snatch.

Slowly and erotically, Devon inched his cock deep inside her wet pussy one delicious inch at a time, making sure to pay special attention to her throbbing g-spot.

"Mmm," moaned Carly. "You are going to make me cum if you keep that up."

"That is my express desire, my love," said Devon who was nearing exquisite orgasm himself.

The two of them made love this way for a while. Finally, both of them reached a climax that literally sent waves of passion throughout both of their bodies. It was a night that neither of them would soon forget, and somehow they knew it would be their last night together for a while.

The next few days were bittersweet for Carly and Devon. They tried to absorb as much of each other as they could. Carly had made the decision to drive home the weekend following her Mom's surprising phone call.

It was Thursday, and Carly had plans to leave the next morning bright and early. Carly packed her things, and Devon gave Carly special attention. He bought her a few odds and ends for her trip. He even told her to lie down while he rubbed her neck and shoulders. It was something special between them. Devon's fingers had a special touch and feel like no other hands in the world as far as Carly was concerned. Carly adored Devon, and in her heart, she knew she always would.

"Carly I love you and I always will," Devon said out of the blue. "I want you to know I will wait for you to return, and I won't give up on our dreams."

"I am so sorry it had to turn out this way, Devon," Carly replied. "I will love you until the day that I die, and I hope we can be together soon again." They held each other close spooning in their bed all night long.

The next morning as the sun peaked through the window, Carly slowly opened her eyes feeling a sadness wash over her like none she had ever felt before. Devon started to rustle, and he held Carly close kissing her neck and giving her one last mini shoulder massage before she had to get up and prepare to leave him.

"Thank you for all you have done for me, Devon. Thank you for loving me," said Carly through sleepy eyes.

"Oh baby come here," and Devon gave Carly a warm, tight embrace.

As Carly pulled away from Devon's driveway, she had a whole melting pot of emotions rolling around inside of her. She was scared to death for her little sister, but she was also afraid she may never see the man she loved again or that he would give up on their dreams. Once Carly reached home, it was a whirlwind of emotions and events for several weeks. She and Devon talked online and on the phone all that they could.

Even though Carly loved Devon more than ever, she couldn't help but wonder if he was truly devoted to her and waiting on her.

These doubts prompted Carly to do something she never thought she would. She decided to do an all-out search on Devon online. She Googled every username she could ever remember him saying he had used on dating and other poetry sites. She also noticed that Devon had recently changed his email password. Carly found that strange since she had always been allowed into his inbox and he was also allowed full access to hers. All of it just didn't add up.

After a week or more of looking for all traces of Devon online, Carly came across something very intriguing. She just happened to be on the poetry site where she and Devon had fallen in love one day and noticed something of interest.

There was a comment by a user that sounded very much like Devon. There was something in the way the user worded their review that sparked Carly's interest. The more

Carly investigated, the clearer it became that this was Devon masquerading as another man on the site that they fell in love and first met! On top of that, it was painstakingly clear that Devon was pursuing another female poet on the site.

The woman even sent Carly a private message, telling her that Devon had said Carly was a jealous ex-girlfriend who meant nothing but to cause him trouble online. Carly was absolutely devastated to put it lightly. Devon wouldn't answer her calls, her texts, or her email. He didn't even have the balls to tell her goodbye. Carly felt like the wind had been knocked out of her. She felt like her life was over. The man she had given her heart to had destroyed her completely. The worst part was that she didn't even get a reason why or hear one word from Devon for weeks.

Slowly, the weeks passed, and Carly tried to go on with her life. Her sister was out of the hospital recovering, and Carly had taken on a new persona on her poetry site so that Devon couldn't haunt her through her poetry.

If she felt like penning a poem, she would sign on as her new persona and then disappear quietly in the background. She still loved Devon and felt as though she would never get over him.

One day, while Carly was writing an article for one of her freelance clients, she heard a bell-like sound on her computer alerting her that a new chat message was coming through. At first, she started to ignore it, figuring it was her client asking her for the article which was due soon. Carly figured she better go see who it was that was buzzing her, and she clicked onto her Hotmail page. Much to her surprise, it wasn't her client at all. It was Devon.

Carly's heart dropped to the floor. My God, it was Devon! What should she do? Should she answer him? Chew him out? Tell him she still loved him? Before she had much time to think about, Carly found herself typing into the little chat box a reply.

She typed the words: Hi, stranger... long time no see.

Devon typed back these words: Carly, I still love you. Will you ever forgive me? I was a complete fool to let you go!

Carly didn't reply immediately. She would have to think about this one for a while. Would she be able to give her heart to Devon again?

9 UNEXPECTED CAPTIVATION

Preface

Heather Shaw was absolutely ecstatic. She couldn't believe that she had landed a job at the prestigious law firm of Lockwood and Murphy in New York City. Heather had graduated top of her class from Columbia University in May. She had immediately set out to find a job as a defense attorney. She had spent nearly 7 years learning her craft, and she was very excited to start using it.

She had applied and sent resumes to at least 20 different law firms in the country. She had interviews at 10 of those and felt pretty good about how they went. Lockwood and Murphy was one of those interviews. The one thing that Heather worried about most was being discriminated against. Heather was not your typical "office girl." She had her own style and was not afraid of self-expression. Heather had always moved to the sound of a different drummer, and that was a fact.

Her appearance at times was a bit daunting for some people. Heather was 23 years old, wore her hair very short in a croppy Emo style, and it was jet black with hot pink streaks.

Heather also had two tattoos and a nose piercing. She was definitely not your typical lawyer type, but she was smart as a whip, and one of the best students to ever attend Columbia University.

She graduated with top honors and came highly recommended by her professors and instructors at law school. Heather had balls and moxie, and she wasn't afraid to use it. Heather was excited as hell to move into her new apartment in New York City this weekend and embark on her new career as a defense attorney at Lockwood and Murphy.

Heather took the subway to work on Monday. She would have to get used to public forms of transportation. She was nervous but very excited about starting her new job at Lockwood and Murphy. She dressed pretty conservatively; she wore a white blouse and a not too short black skirt with black pumps.

When she walked through the door, she got some stares like she always does, but Heather just shrugged it off. She finally found the new office they told her about and started unpacking a few things she had delivered the week before.

Suddenly, she hears a few taps at the door, "Miss Shaw, welcome! So good to see you this morning."

Heather looked up to see a man with the looks of a movie star and the charisma as well. This must be Brad Murphy, she thought to herself. She hadn't met him at the interview, but was told she would be working closely with him.

"Hello, Miss Shaw. I am Brad Murphy, nice to meet you."

Heather extended her hand and said, "Nice to meet you too Mr. Murphy."

"Please feel free to call me Brad," he said. "Get situated in your new office and then come visit me next door here to discuss some things, okay?" said Brad.

"Yes of course," said Heather.

Just then, a buxom bottle blonde with a tight pink skirt on and an even tighter pink tank top walked in. She was plastic from head to toe, but it was easy to see she was as lovable as they came.

"Hi I'm Jenny Clark. I'm the secretary around here. You must be Heather?"

"Yes I am. Nice to meet you Jenny."

"If you need anything, I'll be in the office across the hall," said Jenny.

After unpacking her things, Heather went next door and knocked on Brad's office door. "Come on in," said Brad. "We are glad to have you here, Heather, at Lockwood and Murphy."

"I am glad to be here," said Heather.

She could already tell that the other women

in the office were nuts for Brad. They all swooned when he walked past or said a word. Personally, he wasn't Heather's type at all.

"I have some work for you to do on a case," said Brad. "We have a new client who's has been charged with statutory rape. I'd like you to d-o much of the research and interviewing for this case Heather."

"Sure thing, Brad, I'll help any way that I can," said Heather.

Heather could tell that Brad had a way with the ladies and was used to hearing yes when he asked something. Heather thought he was just a little bit too much of a pretty boy for her liking, though.

She would be working side by side with this man for months. She may as well get used to his handsome good looks she thought.

A couple of weeks had passed and Heather was knee deep involved in this case involving their client Robert James. Heather did not think he was innocent, but she had to spend hours researching and reworking her case. Today, after work, she and Brad were going to work overtime to get ready for the arraignment.

They were trying to get their client out on bail for the length of the trial. Brad and Heather got along great. Brad was kind of intrigued by Heather. She was the only girl he had ever known that didn't throw herself all over him. He was actually kind of sick of women doing that. Heather was growing on him, and he wasn't sure how to handle it.

After everyone else had gone home, Brad and Heather took up residence in Brad's office ready to work on this very challenging case involving all sorts of scandalous and difficult issues. Heather had ordered Chinese take-out, and they heard the delivery boy at the door of the office.

"I've got you covered," smiled Heather, looking at Brad.

Heather paid the nice gentleman, and then, she set up some dinner for both of them at a little table in Brad's office.

"Come eat before it gets cold," said Heather, suddenly feeling like some sort of housewife.

Brad giggled and said, "Yes, honey, I am coming! What did you order me honeybuns?" laughed Brad looking very mischievously at Heather.

Heather did a play hit towards Brad and said, "Okay smarty pants!" as they sat down to eat their General Tso's chicken which was incredibly spicy but wonderfully tasty.

As they were eating, Brad noticed that Heather was really quite beautiful. She had a terrific face. Her complexion was near porcelain, and she had a few sprinklings of freckles that Brad found very sexy.

Ironically, Heather had been thinking similar things about Brad. He had Robert Redford-type looks. He had a boyish face with dimples that would drive any girl crazy, thought Heather. Brad looked up from the last bite of chicken to see Heather gazing at him.

Heather tried to look away really fast before Brad caught her gawking. Brad flashed one of his million dollar smiles that melted Heather dead on the spot.

The sexual tension in the air was starting to build. Heather and Brad both noticed. It was undeniable. It had been building for a couple of weeks now. The two of them had been working closely and feeling the electricity spark between them. They tried to resist it, but it was becoming impossible.

Brad couldn't help but notice Heather's pointed nipples underneath her silk top. Her "bad girl" appearance was incredibly seductive to him. He had never had a girl like this before. He imagined she was a wild cat in bed.

Heather couldn't help but see that Brad had an ample package in his trousers. She could also tell by a man's hands what his penis was like. She had an uncanny ability to do so. She also could see a few times that bulge pressing against the seams of his khaki slacks like it was right this minute.

Heather was getting wet, and she couldn't stop her pussy from reacting. She absolutely could not sit still. Brad had her horny as fuck. Brad noticed her squirming in her seat. That made his dick hurt to be fucked. Neither of them had gotten laid in a while. Heather hadn't been fucked since back in the summer by a friend that was her "fuck buddy," so to speak. Tommy was a good fuck, but Tommy was back home.

Brad hadn't had his cock inside a pussy since his ex-girlfriend Wendy who he fucked in his condo about three months earlier.

Everyone assumed that Brad had a long line of hot women waiting outside his bedroom door, but Brad was choosier than anybody realized. He was searching for something that he had yet to find.

Brad and Heather looked at each other, and the electricity was undeniable and inescapable. Before either of them knew what was going on, they found each other kissing fervently, and without thinking, Brad groped hungrily all over Heather's young, hot body. He grabbed her left ass cheek and pulled her vehemently into his raging manhood.

Brad and Heather were very obviously starved for some hot sex and lusty animal mattress boogie. Brad pulled Heather's blouse down off her shoulder and sucked and licked her shoulders and freckles hungrily and intensely.

"That feels so hot and amazing," said Heather. "Do you think we need to do this?"

Brad answered her while they were kissing, "No we probably shouldn't be, but we are and that's what is so hot. Is it not? Can I fuck you now?" Brad asked.

Heather felt goose bumps cover her entire skin's hot surface. She tingled like sparks of electricity moving through every vein of her gorgeous and curvaceous body. Her flesh craved more. Her appetite was voluminous. She was absolutely starving and parched for the touch and feel of a man taking her to bed and fucking her good and fucking her hard. As awful and desperate as that may sound, that's how Heather felt. She was a passionate woman with raw, unadulterated needs.

Sometimes in our lives, let's face it, lusty sex is the only kind that will quench the animal desires within our aching bodies. This was one of those times, thought Heather, and damn it, she was getting fucked.

Things went from hot to combustible between Heather and Brad. Brad kissed her painstakingly slow from the top of her neck down her neck to her shoulders and upper back. They were ravaging and groping one another's bodies like they were starved for touches, kisses, licks, penetrations, and sucks.

Heather's hot body writhed underneath the super-charged intensity of Brad's hands and fingertips. Suddenly, Heather pushed Brad down on the desk and pulled his pants down to his knees. She went down on his cock fast and furious with all she had within her. His cock was amazingly big and hard for her to fit into her mouth. Heather made gagging sounds as she tried hard to swallow his manhood whole.

"That feels so damn good Heather," said Brad as he pulled her head down on his bulging meat even harder. He was just about to blow his wads when he suddenly said "Why don't you get on top of me and ride my cock, you hot woman?"

"I will fuck you so damn good," said Heather. She climbed on top of him with her hot body and ground into his cock hard and slow. It felt so good to Heather to have a man deep inside of her. Heather started bouncing faster and faster upon his cock until she knew she was going to come all over his lap.

Just then, Heather let out a scream and long heart-throbbing moans and came all over Brad. Brad's balls drew up tight, and he came deep inside Heather, filling her with his sperm.

Heather kind of looked at Brad, and suddenly, they both cracked up in uproarious laughter. "Wow, that was intense," said Heather.

"You aren't kidding!" said Brad who was pretty well spent. "We better get to work on this case huh?" asked Brad.

"Yes we should," replied heather. "Hey Brad can we keep this thing between us quiet?" asked Heather.

"Sure, no problem. In fact, I insist!" Brad said with a sexy grin.

The next day at work was a bit awkward for Heather and Brad. Every time she'd bent slightly over, Brad would try to see her gorgeous brown nipples. When Brad would reach around Heather, she would try as hard as she could to feel his manhood against her ass or thigh.

When they would bump into each other alone in a room, it was obvious these two would be fucking again, and it wouldn't be much longer. Heather could swear she heard Brad moan every time she reached around him for a pencil. He was one horny dick, laughed Heather to herself.

She so much enjoyed Brad's company and not just his body. She also loved his boyish charm and witty personality. There was something deliciously adorable about Brad that Heather knew deep down was growing on her.

After lunch, Heather was walking down the hall to her office, and as she passed Brad's door, she noticed that it was slightly ajar. She heard Brad and a girl's voice coming from inside the door. "How about tonight, you come over and I help you study for that anatomy exam, if you know what I mean?" Brad giggled seductively.

"Brad you are so naughty," said the girl. Heather was just about to barf all over the sculptured carpets in the hallway. She decided to clear her throat real loud to get Brad and the bimbo's attention. Brad quickly turned to see who it was, and he was a bit surprised to see Heather standing there.

"Heather, hey what's up?" Brad asked.

"I just wanted to bring you this file that you needed from the court house."

"Thanks, just put it over there," said Brad. Heather put the file on the table and left as quickly as she could get out of there.

Damn it Heather! She said to herself. Don't do this. He isn't worth it! She had an ongoing mental conversation with herself inside her head. He's the typical guy chasing skirts with no idea how to truly make a woman feel happy and loved. Heather refused to become yet another notch on Brad's belt loop. Heather worked late taking care of some last-minute documents and things on her desktop when she heard footsteps coming down the hall. At first, Heather was startled because she thought she was alone.

"Knock, knock," said Brad. "May I come in?"

"Sure, if you can tear yourself away from Miss Barbie Doll," she replied, annoyed. "You two sure were snuggled closely together."

"Come on, Heather! Chill the fuck out!" replied Brad. "Sherry is simply an old friend from my college days that's all! It means nothing!"

"I don't know why I am being so nuts over this," replied Heather. "It's not like you and I are that serious or anything. Don't worry about it Brad. It's fine. I'm fine," said Heather.

Brad turned Heather around and gave her a warm embrace. "Come on, sweetest! Don't be mad at me please," Brad said and looked up at Heather with huge puppy dog eyes. Who could resist the charm and boyish good looks of Brad? He had a way that grew on all the girls.

Heather found herself craving the invigorating hot touch of Brad. He was all man that was for sure. Heather gave him the once over while he discussed dockets and such things as that. Sorry, but Heather had her mind on more than dockets and judges.

"Excuse me Brad," said Heather. "I need to run to the lady's room if that is okay by you?"

"Sure but hurry back," said Brad in reply. Heather had to go to the little girl's room to cool her wheels just a bit. Damn it! Brad was getting under her usually very tough skin.

Heather was pissed at herself for allowing her mind to go to that very erotic place with Brad. She was having thoughts that would probably get her thrown out of about 40 states in the USA. Heather smiled a smile to herself when suddenly she heard the door to the ladies room open. Who the fuck is that?

She didn't have much time to think before Brad was fucking all over her horny ass. He was kissing her like a crazy man, and she was acting equally as insane. Fuck! thought Brad. This woman is the wildest ride I have ever had in bed.

"You want to take it up a notch baby?" asked a breathless and very turned on Brad.

"Hell, yes!" replied Heather.

Brad kissed and pushed her all the way into the handicapped stall. "Hop up there, and I'll eat you out," said a kinky Brad.

Before she knew what she was doing, Heather had her skirt hiked up standing with each leg on one of those bars that you hold onto to pee. She held onto the bag hanger with her hand. Brad went to town on her shaved pussy like nothing Heather had ever experienced before.

The danger of it only added to the smoking hot experience. The thought of getting caught even heightened the sexual tension and pleasure. The way he licked her snatch drove Heather up the wall, literally.

She gripped around Brad's neck with her

leg and yanked him harder into her creamy pussy. She was rubbing with vehement force her pussy all over Brad's hungry mouth and face. She was just about to come all over him. He had better prepare himself for an unleashing of juice like nothing he had ever tasted.

While he was eating her pussy out, Brad pulled his hard-as-steel cock out from his zipper. It was so hard, it felt as though it might snap in two parts. He beat the fuck out of his cock while a horny Heather creamed him from his nose to his chin and then some.

Heather collapsed down onto the back of the stool and grabbed for brad's face and kissed every drop of her juice off of him.

Heather looked at Brad, smiled and said, "Now that's what I'm saying!" They both laughed and walked out of the bathroom a few minutes later like nothing ever happened.

Over the course of the next three months or so, it was very busy at Lockwood and Murphy law firm. Brad and Heather had won their first big case and were now working on a couple of more together. The whirlwind relationship that they had found themselves in the middle of what was becoming steamier and more exciting by the minute.

Brad had to admit he was totally captivated by Heather Shaw. In fact, Brad had to admit he was falling crazy in love with Heather

Shaw. As surprising as it sounded for playboy Brad to be falling in love with a punk rocker-looking girl like Heather was, it was true. Brad was nuts about her. He knew he might as well face it.

Heather was in love with Brad, too. He was absolutely everything she had never wanted in a man before. That's what made him such a thrill and a challenge to her. Heather had never in her unique existence fallen for a "pretty boy" like Brad, but Brad was no ordinary pretty boy. He was an excellent lover, a terrific friend and funny as hell. He has a passion for law like Heather, and his cock was huge. What more could a girl ask for, really?

The more in love Heather and Brad became, the harder it was to keep their hands off of one another. It was also getting harder and harder to keep their dirty little secret.

They could easily lose their jobs if they were found out. The blonde secretary who had become one of Heather's best friends was the only person who knew about their love affair. They trusted her to keep their hot secret, but no one else could be trusted. That's for sure.

It had become a habit for Heather and Brad to take part in kinky acts of love and lust after hours at the office. They anxiously waited for the night to roll around so they could "work" after hours. There was a sexual force between these two that absolutely never let up.

Finally, everyone started to filter out of the building, and Heather and Brad were beginning to smolder in the intoxicating sexual atmosphere. You could feel the desire hanging like curtains around the edges of the room.

While Brad was finishing up some computer work, Heather decided to have a bit of fun. She snuck into the copy room and pulled her skirt up to reveal her hairless wet snatch. She fingered it ever so tantalizingly slow so as to work it up into a very wet one, so to speak.

When she got her pussy to the meaty lips sticking out like two pink petals ready to open stage, she quit masturbating and sat her ass down on the copier and pressed her lips to the machine like those Garfield pets you see stuck to the back of people's rear view mirrors.

Heather almost came being that spread and splayed upon the machine, but she held back in wanton desire for Brad's dick very shortly. Heather hit the copy button twice so as to get at least two good snapshots of her burning snatch. She cleaned up all traces of her being there and left without a person in the world knowing she was there, at least that's what Heather thought.

When Heather was good and gone, Mr. Lockwood appeared out of the small office in the back with a raging boner in his pants. Fuck, muttered Lockwood under his breath, "That girl got my dick hard as steel," he whispered.

He couldn't believe how mother fucking hot Miss Shaw looked copying a picture of that smoking hot snatch of hers on the copy machine. She looked hot enough to go down on and eat and slurp until every drop of her sweet juice was swallowed.

He started pounding away at his cock just

remembering what she looked like plunging wet fingers in and out her big pussy. He had all the right in the world to fire Miss Shaw of masturbating on the company equipment, but he wouldn't be doing that anytime soon. He hoped to get more glimpses of her goddess-like pussy in the future.

After jerking on his dick about five good pumps, he nearly shot off on his trousers, but decided to savor it a bit more. It was becoming uncomfortable in his pants though.

Mr. Lockwood locked up his office and headed down the hall towards the doors that headed out onto the parking when he heard some incredibly sexy sounds coming from one of the rooms. He followed the sounds until he came to the main conference room with a big oblong table.

He peeked through the cracked door and saw Brad and Heather fucking like two animals in heat. His hand immediately went down to his cock, and he rubbed it through his trousers until he couldn't stand the aching in it anymore. He started wanking his cock harder and harder. The two of them doing it in doggie position was more of a turn on than Mr. Lockwood could stand.

A few more pulls of his cock and a few more visions of Heather's big lips grasping Brad's cock head and he'd shoot all over his suit. Fuck! They looked good getting it on thought Lockwood. Mr. Lockwood was stroking the ever loving fuck out of his long nasty peter. He let out a moan and a nasty groan, but thank God they didn't hear him.

Fuck, she was so hot. He wished he could

put his boner-sized meat inside her big ass snatch. Lockwood was nearly 70 years old, but he still liked getting fucked and eating hot pussy off. One night earlier that week, he had eaten a hairy pussy on a girl that was only19 years old. Damn, her pussy tasted strong and fucking delicious. He writhed and wallowed in her cunt for three solid hours eating the cream out, and the 19 year old squirted all over his horny mouth. Fuck! He closed his eyes and almost blew a wad.

Thinking of that hot little bitch got his boner off quick. He got back to the horny sex at hand with Brad and Heather. He could tell that they were both about to cum everywhere by the way their bodies were twisting and jerking. Lockwood started jacking his cock full throttle now. He was trying to make sure they didn't hear the slapping of his balls as he jerked off.

Finally, the three of them had sweet release. Brad squirted spunk deep inside of Heather, and Lockwood spewed his cream all over his hands and pants. Brad and Heather were kissing and teasing lying on the floor when suddenly they heard a banging noise from the hall.

"What the fuck?" said Brad, sitting up suddenly and getting his pants on to go check out the noise.

Heather had a very worried look on her face as Brad got up to check the hallway. He opened the door and found a cum-soaked Lockwood trying to pick the broken pieces of the urn up he had knocked down in the hall from all of the dirty excitement.

"Lockwood, what brings you here this time of evening?" asked Brad.

"I think the more important question would be for me to ask you that Brad," said Lockwood.

Suddenly, Heather appeared in the hallway.

"Hello Miss Shaw. Fancy meeting you here," said Lockwood in a sultry tone.

"Hi, Mr. Lockwood. Brad and I were just doing some finishing touches on our case for Friday," said Heather.

"Yes, I suppose you were!" chuckled Lockwood who was still trying to wipe the come stains off of his trousers. Heather noticed the come and looked at Brad worried.

"Miss Shaw, you sure looked dynamite splaying your fat pussy all over my copier."

Heather looked shocked, and she turned 10 shades of red.

"You left your musky scent all over my copy machine and the room," said Lockwood as he stroked his cock a bit more under his pants.

Heather felt guilty, but damn it, this guy was getting her hot and wet. Brad could see the sexy look in her eyes, and he felt the beginnings of a boner as well. All three of them could sense the incredible tension in the air.

"Brad, would you mind if I ate this hot lady's meaty pussy off while you watched?"

Brad had always wanted to do that, and he said, "Sure, you can eat the fuck out of it if she doesn't mind."

Heather nodded yes to the proposition, and the three of them went wild with lust. They retreated to Lockwood's office, and Heather stripped down nude except for her heels and sat straight up in Lockwood's big chair. She held both knees up with her arms interlaced underneath them. This gave Lockwood a bird's eye view of this incredible snatch.

"Can I eat your nasty pussy baby?" said Lockwood.

"Eat the fuck out of it now!" cried Heather.

Brad pulled his peter out of his zipper and began to stroke. Lockwood took his time teasing and tickling this big pussy he was feasting on. He first toyed with the lips. Heather could see Lockwood's huge dick as he beat it at the same time. He pulled her lips ever so slowly in his mouth making her squirm with a pleasure and a moan that almost sounded like a whimper.

"I bet if I just flicked the ends of your lips with my tongue real fast you'd pop off," said Lockwood to Heather.

Just saying that to her made her jerk a bit and shoot one squirt all over his face. "Fuck!" said Heather. She damn near pissed at the same time it felt so hot.

"You eat pussy so damn good!" said Heather in a naughty growl.

She then spread her lips and pussy wide open just as far as she could get it to open. She started smearing her snatch all over Lockwood's face. She was jerking and twisting, and Lockwood could hardly keep up with her motion.

He then took the tip of his tongue and flicked very quickly on her big clit and hood. He started to taste white cream ooze out of

Heather's hole. This made him want her pussy badly.

"Can I fuck you now?" asked the naughty Lockwood.

"I insist that you do," said Heather.

Brad nodded yes and was in full swing jerking and rubbing his dick. Lockwood plunged inside of Heather and started banging her. He sloshed in and out of her making them both so damn horny they were going wild. He may be damn near 70, thought Heather, but this man was one hell of a fuck. Lockwood pounded Heather until they all three exploded in an orgasmic chorus that could be heard down the halls.

Afterwards, they all got dressed wondering what they should say or not say to one another. This had been a revealing night to say the least.

"So what's on the agenda for next week?" said Heather.

"I am not exactly sure, but I am almost certain we will have to work hard long hours to make the deadlines," said Lockwood.

"I'm sure we will be up for anything you need us to do, Lockwood," said Brad.

The three of them giggled knowing full well that they would be doing what they had just done time and time again. This truly was an unexpected captivation. They all separated in the parking lot and got into their cars and drove away, all three feeling the beginnings of lustful desire wash all over their bodies.

10 FORBIDDEN CONNECTION

Dead Inside

Ethan McKinley got inside his Mercedes Benz, in the parking lot of General Hospital, in Boston, Massachusetts. He was dead tired. He had, once again, worked two 12-hour shifts, in a row, and he could not wait to get home and take a load off. Ethan was a cardiologist and one of the best in the nation. He was always in demand. He was always saving lives, but still Ethan felt like he was dead inside.

The past year had been one of the very worst in all of Ethan's 40 years of being alive. His soon to be ex-wife, Gloria, was suing Ethan for everything she could get her hands on, including their precious son, Justin, who was 2 years old. She was claiming emotional abuse because of Ethan's affair with his colleague, Susan Brendon. It was true, Ethan had a short-lived affair with Susan, but he stopped the affair and had no intention of looking back. He knew it was wrong and told Gloria so. Ethan was a good man, but he had weakened with Susan. He was working excruciating hours at the hospital and was lonely. Susan was gorgeous and smart, and he fell for the temptation. Also, his wife had become angry and bitter. It seemed, all that she wanted from Ethan was his money. He was convinced, now, that was the only reason Gloria even married him.

Of course, Gloria held the affair against him and was milking it for everything it was worth. The truth was, Ethan had stopped the affair and, even to this day, was not seeing anyone. He was lonely and frustrated, and missed seeing Justin whenever he wanted to. Finally, Ethan pulled into the driveway of his modest house. He had even let Gloria stay in their 2-story dream home, so that Justin would be comfortable. She had all of the amenities: a pool, hot tub, fancy appliances, a 2-car garage, and a deck. Ethan had even bought her a brand new Lexus, on her birthday, 6 months before she decided she wanted a divorce.

Now, Ethan found himself embroiled in an ugly divorce and, seemingly, one with no end. He was lonely, hurt, and saddened by the whole wretched ordeal. He had no one, really, that he could depend on. His family all lived in California. He had come out East to study Cardiology and had decided to stay there, after graduation, because of the higher pay and better jobs.

Ethan unlocked the door to his one story,

3-bedroom home. It was very modest, but still nice. He tripped on his golf clubs, walking through the door, and cursed out loud. He made his way to the kitchen. "Boy Ethan, this place is a wreck." He muttered to himself. He opened the fridge because he was absolutely starving to death. He saw that there was nothing worth eating, except some moldy cheese and a few slices of ham. Shit, he was fucking starving. Ethan got on the phone and ordered a delivery pizza. Then, he sat down, to watch a few shows on TV, except the remote was nowhere to be found. That's it, he thought to himself. Tomorrow, I post an ad and try to find someone to help out around here.

The next morning, Ethan woke up, dog tired. He took a quick shower and faced the fact that he didn't have any clean shirts to put on. Then, it dawned on him. "Oh yeah!" He thought. "I am going to run an ad today, online, for a housekeeper." Ethan grabbed a stale piece of bread and made himself a quick piece of toast and a cup of instant coffee. Then, he grabbed his laptop and went to work on his ad. He placed his ad for a live-in housekeeper, in several of the top online sites. He was hoping for a bite soon, because he needed a woman's touch around his place and he needed it quickly! Thank God he was off work for the next couple of days. Maybe, that would be enough time to find someone to help out. He didn't care if Gloria liked it. It was time he did something for himself, for a change.

Ethan spent the day doing a bit of grocery shopping and tending to his plants, outside. He also took a long nap, which was much needed. Just when he was about to give up on hearing any replies from his ad, his cell phone rang.

"Hello," said Ethan.

"Yes, hi. I am calling about your ad for a housekeeper," Said a woman with a sultry, almost Jamaican sounding, accent.

"Yes, I am glad that you called. Would you mind coming over for an interview, in about an hour?" asked Ethan.

"Sure thing," she said. Ethan gave her his address and told her he would be looking forward to meeting her.

Jadan drove up to the house and was a bit nervous about her interview. She wanted to make a good impression, but she was very different from the people here, in Boston. She was originally from Jamaica, but had come to the states to attend college. Jadan was very smart, but she wasn't able to go to college and survive financially. When she found out about her father's sickness, back home, she started to work, to help her mom out with her younger brothers and sisters. Her parents were very poor, so Jadan decided to start cleaning houses, to help them survive. She hoped to go back to the University one day, though.

Jadan knocked on Ethan's door, very nervously, not knowing what to expect, exactly. He opened the door and the two of them locked eyes, instantly. Jadan thought that Ethan was very handsome and his smile was absolutely breathtaking. Jadan smiled back and shook Ethan's hand. He couldn't believe the beauty of this woman standing in his doorway. Her skin was a radiant chocolate color that looked as smooth as velvet. Her hair was a beautiful silky black that appeared almost blue.

"Come on in and let's talk a little bit." Said Ethan, showing Jadan inside and around the house. He showed Jadan where things were and where she would reside, should he decide to give her the job cleaning. Ethan asked her about her life and she told him about her college days, and how she was now helping her mom, back in Jamaica.

"Maybe, someday, you can go back to school and finish your education. It is never too late you know," said Ethan.

"I guess it is always possible," said Jadan. It seemed ridiculous, but the two of them felt very comfortable together. It was fairly obvious that there was chemistry between them that couldn't be denied.

"Jadan, you have the job," said Ethan. "I have a good feeling about you."

"Thank you very much!" said Jadan.

"Why don't you go get your things, come back, and set up, in your room, maybe, we can have dinner and get to know each other a little better," said Ethan.

"Okay, I will be back in an hour, or so."

Ethan thought she was absolutely charming and extremely beautiful. He couldn't help it. He just did. While she was getting her belongings, Ethan whipped them up some salads and a little bit of soup. He took it out, on the deck, so that they could enjoy a bit of night air.

About an hour later, Ethan heard Jaden drive up in the driveway, in her Volkswagon bug. He went outside and helped her bring her things in. She went to her quarters and put some of her things away. Then, Ethan invited her out to the balcony for a light supper. They talked about their lives and growing up, while they ate and they both continued to feel amazingly comfortable. Ethan discussed all of the ins and the outs of the job, and Jaden made it clear she understood what was expected of her.

In fact, Jadan demanded he let her pick up the mess and clean the kitchen. Ethan couldn't help but watch her, as she moved gracefully. Ethan was quite enamored with this dark skinned beauty. She had a rare beauty and a rare personality. After cleaning the kitchen, Jadan started a load of Ethan's laundry washing.

"Thank you much, Jadan. You didn't have to start tonight," said Ethan.

"Sure I did," smiled Jadan. "You hired me to clean and I will."

The two of them turned in that night and the next morning, Jadan was up early, preparing breakfast for Ethan. Ethan came downstairs, rubbing his eyes and sniffing in the air. He said, "What smells so delicious, Jadan?"

"It's my specialty, Eggs Benedict," she replied. Ethan sat down and she got him a plate with some delicious piping hot coffee and fresh orange juice.

"Thank you so much, Jadan. This is delicious," he said.

"It's the least I could do, considering you gave me a job and a room to live in," Jadan replied.

"I need to get to the hospital, but I'll be home in time for dinner," Ethan replied with a wink.

Jadan spent the entire day cleaning, then cooking a delicious spicy jerk chicken recipe, with rice pilaf and homemade bread. When Ethan walked through the door that evening, the house smelled delicious and looked even better. Jadan walked into the living room and Ethan couldn't believe his eyes. She looked gorgeous!

"You look incredible, Jadan," said Ethan.

"Thank you," she replied. Jadan was wearing a simple, hot pink tube top dress, but the color set off her deep skin beautifully. The outfit kept her cool, so Jadan thought there was no harm in wearing it. Of course, it is possible she subconsciously put it on to turn

Ethan's head a little bit.

"You have about 15 minutes before dinner is complete, if you want to get cleaned up" Jadan said.

"Okay, I will be down shortly." said Ethan. He went upstairs, showered, and shaved.

Ethan emerged from upstairs just about the time Jadan had dinner on the table. They sat down together and enjoyed Jadan's delicious cooking. "You cook superbly," said Ethan.

"Thank you, Ethan," she replied. She couldn't help but stare at Ethan's dark, wavy hair and beautiful olive skin. He truly was a hunk. Neither of them realized it, but they had, neither one, been in an interracial relationship before. It seemed as if there were sparks in the air between them. There was definitely a noticeable chemistry. They were both getting highly aroused by one another, but didn't know what to do about it, or whether to even do anything about it.

Jadan got up and started to clear the dishes, and take them to the sink to wash. Ethan helped her. Jadan could feel him slightly brush against her back and it turned her on, immensely. It had been several months since she had made love to a man. It had been several months for Ethan, as well. Jadan turned around, from washing dishes and there was Ethan right in her face.

He started to kiss her, before he knew what hit him. Jadan returned the kiss, passionately and hungrily. She had never wanted a man as badly as she wanted Ethan, now. Ethan laid her back on the kitchen table and started to bang her hard and furious. Jadan put her long dark legs up, by his ears, revealing her hot, pink labia and clit to him.

"Fuck, you have a beautiful pussy. It is so pink and wet," said Ethan, as he began to plow her. He could hear and see his hard cock going in and out of her nasty snatch.

She moaned with extreme pleasure. Then, she said to Ethan, "I want to go down on your cock and lick my juices off of it." So, that is exactly what she did, she went down on his dick, balls deep. She licked, sucked, and drug her tongue all around the rim, just tempting Ethan to squirt. He loved how her tongue did little flicks all over his cock head. It drove him wild. Jadan fingered her snatch, while she went down his dick. It looked nasty, seeing her fingers plunging in and out of her deep, wet pussy. He could hear how drenched it got and it made him nearly cum.

She rose up from his dick, and crammed one of her huge brown nipples right in his mouth. She sucked the other tit at the same time. Watching him suck one was a massive turn on as well.

"Why don't we go outside and fuck. Let's dare to get caught?" said Jadan.

That was a kinky idea, but Ethan loved it. Maybe they could go out in the driveway and fuck in his car. Jadan loved the idea. So, they went out to his car and cracked a couple of windows, in hopes of, maybe, being heard by the neighbors.

Jadan got on top of him, cowgirl style, and rode him hard and wild. She'd rise completely up, then, slam her pussy down on his cock, making it stand straight up like a steel rod.

Every time she thrust down upon his throbbing dick, it would hurt a bit more to spurt and squirt. But, Jadan knew what she was doing and she didn't dare let that horny cock squirt, yet.

"I am going to ride you reverse cowgirl, now, baby!" said Jadan. When it came to sex, Jadan knew what she was doing. She was a complete wildcat in the bedroom. She motioned for Ethan to take her inside, so that they could fuck in the bed. Little did they know, they had a voyeur.

The man next door had been watering his lawn and heard them screwing. It turned him on so much, his cock got too big for his shorts. So, he pulled it out the side hole and jerked the fuck out of it, while they screwed. Damn, his cock felt horny. He pulled his dick off, real hard, and it squirted off all over the lawn.

When they got inside, Jadan mounted Ethan's dick, reverse cowgirl, and rode him hard as fuck! Ethan loved the view, when Jadan screwed him reverse cowgirl. She was hotter than hot and turning him the fuck on. He could see her meaty lips pull up and down on his hurting dick, as she slid up and down on it. Of course, when he said hurting, he meant only in the best sort of way. Suddenly, Jadan was ready to mix it up, again. She said to Ethan, "Why don't I lie with my head hanging backwards, off of the bed. You can come up, behind me, and ram that dick down my throat?"

Jadan leaned back and hung her gorgeous head off the bed and took his entire girth deep down her throat. He could have cum in one stroke, or suck, but he pulled out, because he wanted to unload in her nasty, hairy pussy. He hadn't had a hairy one in a while, and she had a mass of furr on her big pussy.

"How about you fist me Ethan?" asked Jadan.

"I will try, if that is what you want," he said. So, Jadan sat straight up, on the bed, and began to squirm on his thumb and forefinger. Fuck! He could feel her lips grip his fingers and it felt awesome. Slowly, he slid his middle finger deep in her hairy snatch. She started begging for more fingers, so he buried them inside her and she took them all, down to his wrist. She fucked his fist, until she about squirted. Then, she slowly pulled her pussy off, as her lips grabbed his hand and he, immediately, plunged his hard as a rock dick deep inside her. It only took them both a few minutes to cum, with mind blowing orgasms that rocked the entire room. For Ethan, it felt so fucking good cumming deep inside her hairy pussy.

After their wild sexual adventure, the two of them collapsed into bed, chatting and laughing, like they had been together for years.

"I hope I didn't overstep," said Jadan.

"No way did you overstep. I attacked you, remember?" he said, tickling her at the same time. "I think we have a natural chemistry, Jadan, and the sex was amazing.

"I do feel as though I should warn you about my soon to be, ex-wife, Gloria." Ethan filled Jadan in on all of the details and the bad stuff that happened between them. Jadan felt terrible!

Ethan and she wished she could help him somehow. "Let's just, not let on that we are involved in a spicy and very sexy relationship, okay?" said Ethan.

"Of course not!" smiled Jadan. The two of them laughed and talked about their lives, until they fell asleep in each other's arms.

The next morning, the alarm clock seemed to go off unusually early. Ethan certainly didn't want to get up and go to the hospital, and Jadan felt all warm and toasty, snuggled up to him. However, he knew he had to, eventually. First, though, he couldn't resist planting a long, hot kiss upon Jadan's gorgeous ruby lips. Jadan let out an early morning moan and kissed him back, with great passion and longing. Before they knew it, they were both allowing themselves to be pulled into the fury of hot lovemaking and gushing delights.

Jadan pushed Ethan's dark head down, between her amorous thighs, to her love box. "Eat your breakfast, babyb" she said, as she arched her furry snatch up, to his hungry mouth.

"Fuck, that feels hot as hell!" Jadan whimpered. Her pussy pretty much stayed hot and horny. She was only 27 years old and very vital. Ethan wallowed in her nectar and hair, eating up every loving spoonful of Jadan's horny-ass cunt.

She popped up, on top of him, and rode him slow and seductively. She did figure 8 grinding motions all over Ethan's cock infested lap. His dick stood straight up, and Jadan would pull all the way up and slam down, on it. She made sure that, on her way down, his dick head rubbed her g-spot just right. This caused her pussy to produce cream and loads of it!

"Fuck, that feels so damn hot on my g-spot. I am going to gush everywhere if you keep this up," she said.

Jadan started to suck her own tits, vigorously. She wished she could still get in the position to lick her own clit like she used to. "That would turn him on big time," she thought! He melted with desire, while his cock raged with an eternal fire. She was slowly sliding down, feeling his cock throb within her pussy, making her more juicy than Jadan thought possible.

She was getting close to cumming all over his big, white dick and his dick was prepared to squirt right back. They both started to have an orgasm and Jadan let out a scream that said she was feeling no pain. They writhed, in total ecstasy, for a few mintues, then, landed in each other's arms.

A little while later, Jadan made Ethan breakfast number two and he was out the door, on his way to the hospital. Jadan went to the market that day and bought some special steaks for grilling. She was dreading the fact that Gloria might come over. She hoped she could act like she was only his maid and nothing more.

11 FORBIDDEN CONNECTION 2

Surprising News

Jaden looked at the stick in disbelief, yet excited and surprised all at the same time. Could she be seeing correctly? Was she really pregnant with Ethan's child? It seemed impossible to be true. She never thought it was that easy for a woman to conceive. She had always heard it took 3 or 4 months at least. She really hoped that her pregnancy wouldn't put a damper on the incredibly hot sex she and Ethan had been sharing.

Jaden couldn't wait until Ethan got home from the medical clinic where he had been volunteering since his arrival in Jamaica. She and Ethan had enjoyed a whirlwind romance like the kind you only read about or see in movies. They shared an unbelievable amount of passion for each other. The mere thought of him made her tingle. Thinking of that first night brought a flood of emotions. She could still feel him in her arms and as he slipped his stiffness deep inside her. It was as if she could see his desire grow with every kiss they shared. There were so many things she remembered about that night, and everything only made her love him more.

Jaden didn't think it was possible for two people to be this much in love. It started as animal lust, but it didn't take long before they realized they needed one another desperately. She needed his strength. He needed her tenderness. They had both had a rough few years and falling into one another's arms seemed inevitable.

As Jaden lay down upon their soft comforter, her mind drifted back to the memories of their sudden romance and how he had whisked her off her feet. He had treated her body to the most exciting lovemaking and hot sex she had ever experienced. When Ethan ran his long fingers along her ebony flesh, she came alive. It felt like tiny sparks of electricity filled her body from head to toe. She is so surprised when Ethan followed her to Jamaica. He was from Boston back in the States, and he wasn't accustomed to island life at all, but he had adjusted so well. She was very proud of him.

She knew how hard it was to go to a brand new area and try to start a new life among the unknown customs. She lay awhile dreaming about how much Ethan had given up as a heart surgeon to come here and work in the clinic just to be with her. She also thought about how evil his ex-wife Gloria had been. She would stop at nothing to destroy their lives together. Jaden had almost drifted off to sleep when she felt pair warm arms in wrap around her from behind.

"Mmm... Hi baby, how did work go?" said Jaden sleepily.

"It went well, but I am extremely happy to be in bed with the most beautiful woman in the world right now."

Jaden pulled Ethan's body into her and kissed him back with a passion like no other. She was starved for his kiss. She adored him, and she craved him with an animal lust and the purest of love of all rolled into one. Ethan got on top of his wife and straddled her lean dark body. The moonlight glistened through the lace curtains casting a glow over her beautiful face. Ethan pulled his cock in and out of his lover all the while looking into her eyes and thinking how lucky he was to have Jaden. She was the most amazing and sexy woman he had ever known.

They made love for what seemed like hours. Her folds pulled him inside as like a knife into a wet leather sheath. Her cunt gulped him down greedily as if it was drinking the finest nectar. Her pliant wet lips greedily inched their way up along his throbbing cock. Her lips were velvet-tipped wings that brushed his shaft with endless waves of shudders filled with moans and desire. The night seemed to drift into another dimension as Ethan and Jaden drank the kisses of desire in with every delicious joining of their lips. Their tongues danced the dance of sweet seduction as their bodies mimicked the motion and rhythm. When they exploded into orgasmic ecstasy, they did so at the same time and then collapsed lovingly into each other's arms falling into a peaceful and secure sleep.

Jaden's Good News

The next morning, the two of them awoke still woven in each other's arms. They opened their eyes to the reason each of them even drew a breath. They were so much in love and so happy it seemed as if nothing on earth had the power to destroy it. They could both be happy for the rest of their lives being loved by the other.

Jaden got up and prepared some coffee, eggs, and toast: Ethan's favorite breakfast. He had to be at work in about an hour, and Jaden wanted to be the perfect wife. She wanted to make Ethan feel like a king.

Ethan came into the kitchen and hugged Jaden from behind also nuzzling her neck and planting kisses on her nape. It gave Jaden goose bumps and she loved it. Ethan also rubbed up and down her spine showing Jaden how much he cared for her and her comfort. It had become a custom most every morning sort of a thing between them, and Jaden had come to look forward to it.

The two of them sat down and enjoyed breakfast by the window they loved sitting at. They could see the turquoise blue waves splash upon the shore and see the palm trees dance in the breeze while they enjoyed each other's company and their breakfast together. About halfway into the meal, Jaden suddenly became queasy. She had to excuse herself and go to the restroom. Ethan knocked lightly at the door asking her what was wrong.

"I'm fine Ethan. I just got a little upset to my stomach that's all."

Ethan went to the kitchen and got Jaden a cool towel. The two of them sat down on the sofa while Ethan applied the towel to Jaden's head and throat.

"Jaden, are you sure you are okay, darling? You looked a bit woozy right before you got up from the table."

Ethan looked worried.

"Ethan, there is something I need to tell you. Baby, I just found out yesterday and I hope you are okay with the news. I took a pregnancy test today that I picked up at the drug store and it came up positive. I am pregnant with our child!"

"Oh my God, that's wonderful Jaden!" He hugged her in a warm embrace. "I wish you had told me sooner. How long have you known?"

"I just found out last night. I am so happy Ethan! I was hoping you would be, too."

"Baby of course I am ecstatic. You're carrying our child. How could I not be?"

They were both beside themselves with the news. They talked about it for the rest of the afternoon planning on how they'd raise their child, what doctors she would see, and finding a larger place to live.

Ethan gave her a passionate kiss goodbye and she felt a little woozy so she went to lie back down for a while. As she drifted off to sleep, she began to have a nightmare. The dream was about a true experience that had happened to her. It had a way of coming back to haunt her. It had happened to her only six years earlier; it was the single most devastating experience of her life. It had turned her world upside down, and she had never told another living soul. It was embarrassing and painful all at the same time. She couldn't stand having flashbacks of the horrific night. She even more hated thinking about the levels she sunk to during that painful time of her life.

It was a time she would just as soon forget, but her mind wouldn't let her. It had simply been far too traumatic. Just when she thought she had put it out of her mind, the memories came flooding back. They especially seemed to haunt her dreams.

She could see flashes of the face, the humiliating experiences, and the evil that ensued afterwards. It usually became too much for her and she awakened drenched in sweat. This time proved no different. Jaden sat straight up in bed trembling, and she finally got her bearings straight and remembered she was in her bed.

Jaden went to the bathroom and was ill again. This was normal morning sickness, and she knew it so she forced down a piece of dry toast and juice. She could tell that Ethan was so happy about her pregnancy. This made her feel wonderful. She and Ethan had talked about how much he wanted a child. Gloria, his ex-wife, wasn't able to have kids, and this had greatly disappointed Ethan.

Jaden actually had no idea how happy

Ethan was. He thought about Jaden and their upcoming child all day while working at the medical clinic. This type of work was so different for him compared to his former career as a heart doctor in Boston. The people here were so poor and very appreciative of any little thing he did for them. It gave Ethan such satisfaction to know he was truly helping someone that if not for his help might be very ill or even die.

It was obvious these people truly needed him, and that gave Ethan a sense of accomplishment he hadn't had in a long time. Ethan was a doctor truly driven by what he could give his patients, not so much by what he could get from them. His patients truly came to love him for his caring and considerate ways. His bedside manner was impeccable, and he was more than just liked by everyone who came to see him. Ethan was a "patient's doctor" and for good reason: he truly cared.

An Unexpected Visitor

Ethan drove home so excited to see his beautiful wife. Just like on the first night they met, Ethan walked up behind Jaden, who was preparing salad, and began to plant sweet and warm kisses all along the nape of her neck and her shoulders. He saw goose bumps form beneath her flesh. He knew what that meant. It meant if he were to slip two fingers under her skirt, he would discover a drenched chocolate snatch dying for him to enter into with his throbbing muscle.

Jaden tried to act nonchalant, but she

couldn't before she lifted her right leg up by Ethan's hip just begging for him to thrust it deep within her. There was always such a sensuous eroticism about fingering her juicy cunt while he kissed her. He loved how, when his fingers slipped inside her quivering pussy, she moaned and gasped into his mouth as their tongues probed each other's tongues. She truly loved his fingers in her creamy cunt, but she always wanted more than just fingers. She craved his cock more than any woman he had ever had, and so he had married her.

She groped to unzip him so that his dick could spring out of his zipper with readiness. Jaden had noticed her libido seemed to be getting stronger. It was the hormones raging within her hot body swelling her cunt to soft pink proportions and making her swollen nipples puff out. He always watched her hand on him with a tender lust in his eyes as he pictured her guiding his cock into her mouth or pussy. Ethan had always been amazed by how her cunt seemed to swallow his shaft eagerly. Her breath would become almost hesitant as his balls pressed up against her ass between her wide spread legs. Her need to be satisfied was almost constant as of late, always so willing to be pleasured and to return it threefold. It was hard to determine which needed him more, her aching nipples, her demanding cunt, or her yearning eyes.

As Jaden and Ethan headed to their soft bed, they simply knew that they needed each other in every possible way imaginable. Each thrust of Ethan's hard cock inside Jaden brought a moan to her lips. Each moan seemed to blend into the next until she sounded as if the pleasure was nearly an unending torture. There was never a moment when her entire body felt as good as when Ethan was plunging slowly into her depths while his mouth was caressing hers or her neck. They fit together like a hand in a glove, and that made them what they were, simply in love.

Ethan could feel her inner folds tightening around his cock as her moans turned into grunts of desire that always told him she was about to cum. Her fingernails dug into his back, her heels dug into his ass and pulled him deeper with each thrust. He knew she wanted him to bathe her pussy with his thick seed at that precise moment when her juices exploded from inside her. It was all he could do to keep from cumming before her; whenever he could feel it happening, he would lean forward and passionately kiss her. Her mouth was always hungry for his and readily accepted his tongue on hers.

Her ass rose up off the bed and his hands slipped beneath it. Clutching her cheeks firmly but gently always told Jaden his explosion was moments away and she would wiggle her ass from side to side to rub her clit against his coarse pubic hair, something that always made her cum hard and fast.

Ethan looked down to see Jaden's hard clit glow almost an angry red before him. He felt his balls tighten and arched his back as he drove his ramrod deep into her quivering cunt. Jaden cried out as she felt his seed filling her pussy with a liquid molten fire of his creamy cum. She gave one final thrust back and her pussy went into ecstatic spasms as again and again; her cum soaked his crotch. She would almost nearly pass out when she had these immense orgasms, and lately it seemed they all were. The two of them collapsed into each other's safe and secure arms. The next morning, Jaden woke up early for some reason she thought it was just another symptom of the hormones.

Jaden wanted to unwind this morning so she ran a warm lavender bubble bath. It is supposed to be calming and soothing. As the bubbles began to froth like white clouds, Jaden slipped her ebony legs out of her pale pink camisole set. When she dipped her toes into the warm bathtub, she noticed her breasts were plump and juicy like two ripe plums. Even the slightest brush of one across fabric or anything sent orgasmic shocks through her hormone-raging body. This seemed to be a major plus side of being pregnant.

As she let the water envelop her body, Jaden became increasingly more turned on and warm all over. The ripples of water kissed her skin with moisture and the feelings of ecstasy seemed to fall over her from head to toe. She let the warm water wash over her and lead her into the throes of pleasure.

Her hand made its way down between her ebony thighs, and she felt the moistness of her curly muff as she inserted her middle finger into her cunt. Her fingers curled inside her oozing pussy and tenderly grazed across her swollen g-spot. Her hips thrust into her hand driving her hard clit against the heel of her delicate hand. She closed her eyes and thought of Ethan's proud hard cock glancing off the edges of her throbbing g-spot. She added another finger inside her gripping pussy and slowly twisted them inside her.

She pictured riding Ethan's straining love muscle as she wiggled herself down onto it. She so loved to ride his cock, and the mere thought of it buried deep inside her made her fingers begin to pump faster and faster in and out of her sucking hole. She reached down with her other soapy hand and began to squeeze her breast, her fingers twisting and pulling on the hard nipple, the sensations rippling through her body like electricity. She leaned back against the tub her hips pumping into her hand, her eyes closed as she moaned picturing Ethan pounding away at her frothy cunt in the hot water. She pulled her fingers out just before she came to drag then up and down her swollen slit teasing herself into frenzy her ass lifting up off the bathtub floor exposing her heated cunt to the cooler air above the water. Her clit was swollen and her lips bulging around her finger. As she arched her back and moaned loudly, she drove three fingers deep into her protesting cunt. Frantically, she pumped her pussy onto her fingers, her cunt gripping at her fingers as they plunged in and out of her. It didn't take long before Jaden was exploding in a hot orgasm that seemingly swept over her entire body. Just as she was lost in the ecstasy of it, she looked up to see Ethan watching her with a look of pure love and lust in his eyes.

Jaden leaned over to Ethan and began to suck his cock like she was starving. Ethan had always felt that Jaden sucked him off better than anyone. Her mouth felt like a velvet blanket wrapped around his cock. She moved up and down his shaft slowly and assuredly looking up at him with dark ebony eyes that always melted Ethan's heart when she looked at him. It wouldn't matter if they were married for 50 years, he would never tire of her blowjobs. The way she sucked his cock was beyond unbelievable. It was absolutely the best he had ever had. Jaden had always known how to handle his cock from day one. She knew just the right touches, the strength for which to suck, and she never failed to swallow each and every drop.

One of Ethan's favorite things to do was to look down on her ebony eyes as she sucked. She looked up at him with animal lust and pure love within them. This made the intensity and the enjoyment of it even more exciting. The way his wife handled his throbbing muscle was as if she had in her hands and mouth the most precious thing in the world to her. Right before he would come, she would hold his hardened balls within her hands daring them to release their thick seed. The combination of the silken lapping of her tongue and her hands on his balls made him spew every time.

Once the first wad of seed was released from his cock Ethan watched closely as it slid down her throat and watched his wife gulp and swallow. He could almost hear it hit the back of her greedy throat. He adored the look that came into her dark eyes as she tasted the very first drop. It didn't matter what they did together, it was a special experience. Not only did they have mind-blowing sex, they also walked hand in hand along the beach filled with the most comforting and amazing feeling two people could share. Ethan had never believed in soul mates before, and he actually used to believe it was a bunch of bull, but that was before he met his incredible wife who was the love of his life. The comfort they shared was as soothing and yet exciting as anyone could imagine.

Haunted By The Past

Ethan gave Jaden a long and romantic kiss before he headed to the clinic or another day's work. He bent down and gently patted her tummy and kissed it as well. She was carrying the most precious thing in the world to Ethan. His ex-wife Gloria couldn't give Ethan a child and that had always been a thorn in his side. It was a huge part of the reason their marriage didn't work out and probably why Ethan did stray that one time. That was why Gloria seemed bound and determined to make him pay for maybe the rest of his life.

Gloria had made Ethan's life a living nightmare ever since he made the mistake of adultery. He had quit and truly tried to be faithful to her. But Gloria was eaten up with bitterness and resentfulness. Even if Ethan hadn't cheated on her, the marriage was destined or failure. Looking back, Ethan realized that he never really loved Gloria, and he knew for sure she never loved or cared about him. He and Gloria had probably the ugliest divorce ever. Ethan had a successful practice as a heart surgeon and physician at Boston General Hospital, and he and Gloria had a beautiful home in the suburbs. By the time she got through with him, he hardly had anything left.

Ethan was a good man and freely gave up everything to make up for the pain he had caused Gloria, but it wasn't enough. She was hell bent on making him pay. It seemed the more he gave into her and shelled out the money, the greedier she became. Ethan now wondered if she ever truly was hurt by his adultery or she simply just used it as an excuse to milk him for everything he had worked for. But now, Ethan had finally found happiness in the arms of Jaden and nothing was going to destroy that. He wouldn't let it.

Jaden spent her morning thinking about preparations for the new baby; she called and made a doctor's appointment and then started looking online for some cute ideas for nursery décor. She got lost browsing the different sites when she was startled suddenly by the phone ringing. She got up from her lazy comfort at the PC and went to answer the call. She assumed it was Ethan and answered very happily and almost excitedly. She was surprised to hear a woman's voice at the other end.

"Is this Jaden... the whore who married the rich doctor from Boston?" said the woman's muffled voice on the other end.

"Who is this?" asked Jaden very suspiciously.

"This is someone who knows all about your sordid past, Jaden. I don't just know bits and pieces, but I know everything you did. All of the shameful filthy things you did."

The evil voice continued.

"I wonder how Ethan would feel about the fact that his sweet little Jamaican wife had once sold her pussy for money. You are nothing but a disgusting whore with a diseased cunt, you bitch! And before I am done with you, Ethan will know every little thing you did with your pussy. He'll know all of the deceitful lies you have been telling him. He will know he has married nothing but a useless street whore with a cunt that has seen more cocks than lives on your tiny island. Face it, you disgusting slut; your marriage is over. What a pity, too... you being pregnant with his baby and all. Oh well, you win some, you lose some."

The evil voice was laughing as the receiver suddenly went dead with an eerie click.

Jaden was in a state of shock as her black eyes filled with hot tears. She thought she had kept her dark secret under wraps and that no one would ever find out that she was kidnapped and forced into all sorts of vile sexual behavior. She had never told another soul. It was a pain and darkness that she carried like a scarlet letter. It haunted every day of her life. She had felt dirty as a woman and worthless as a person. The flashbacks never stopped. The only time she had ever felt alive since the awful events that had destroyed her happened was when she met Ethan, the only man who had ever truly cared.

If and when he found out about this, he would be devastated. Ethan was a traditional man in many ways. He wanted the wife who baked him cakes and pies, the white picket fence lined with tulips, and the little boy who would come racing out the door each evening into his arms begging him to play ball. Jaden didn't have any idea what to do. She felt as though her life was crashing down like a stone wall all around her. She allowed the black cloud that had loomed silently in the background for six years overtake her, and she laid down on the sofa and cried the tears she never really had cried before.

Ethan had just signed onto his laptop at the clinic to look up a medication he had questions about, before prescribing it to a very sick little boy. He saw his email blinking and he smiled to himself thinking it must be his beautiful and imaginative wife. He even looked around him in case she had sent him a preview of what he was having for dessert later. Ethan couldn't resist. He would never tire of seeing Jaden's gorgeous body. He opened his email and clicked onto the first new email.

As Ethan read the vile words before him, he almost fainted. He was in complete shock and wasn't sure how to react. He quickly went to the exam room and gave the little boy's mom the prescription and then locked the clinic door. He somberly went back into his office and read the rest of the anonymous letter. It was all about Jaden. The things that were said about her were almost too painful for Ethan to read. He broke down into tears and felt like he had been stabbed in the gut with a dagger. He had no idea if they were true, who sent the vicious mail or anything. At that moment, Ethan didn't know a damned thing. His mind, heart, and soul were completely blank and destroyed.

He barely caught his breath, when he remembered there was one more new email to open and it appeared to have attachments. He was terrified to open it, but then again he knew he must. He swirled with every emotion a man could have. He was sad, angry, jealous, and livid. He had never felt this way before in his entire life. When he finally got the nerve to click on the email, Ethan had no idea of what he was about to see. Little did he know that at that very moment, he would gone through the most traumatic few minutes of his life. The pictures and video were so obscene he got physically sick. He saw his beautiful Jaden bound, bloody, bruised, and being treated like an animal.

She had been marketed in videos taunting her as the whore who would fuck anyone or anything. There were photos of various objects of all shapes and sizes being thrust inside of her cunt. Even as evil as it sounds, she was smiling in many of the pictures and for a perverted or just kinky movie buyer she seemed to enjoy her lifestyle and her "movie" career. At first, Ethan thought about how he was going to divorce her immediately. Then he started to think. There has got to be more to this story. There had to be an evil person behind this. He knew his wife and she was nobody's whore or slut. She was a beautiful woman inside and out. The devoted and loyal man in Ethan was never giving up on his bride and the mother of his child. No one could ever turn him against Jaden. He loved her that much.

At that moment, Ethan knew he had better drive home and take Jaden into his arms and never let her go. He was bound and determined to find justice for her. He was ashamed of himself that he even doubted her for a second. He locked up the clinic and raced home to his wife. If anything, he knew he loved Jaden more, on that ride home, than he ever had before. Ethan quickly pulled up into the driveway and he noticed the door was ajar. That's odd, he thought, Jaden wouldn't do that. She was very careful about things like that. She had lived a rough life and in some rough neighborhoods. He had never known her to fail to lock a door... never.

A pit formed in Ethan's gut and the whole story started taking shape before his eyes, and he knew at that moment who was responsible for dredging up this evil against him and Jaden. Ethan raced out of the car and bound through the front door. He didn't see anything at first and then he heard voices from his and Jaden's bedroom.

When he got to the door of the bedroom, his heart nearly stopped cold. There was Jaden bound like in the email pictures, and she had a bloody nose and a black eye. Then he saw her. Gloria stood over Jaden with a pistol pressed between her eyes spouting off cruel and vicious words. Ethan froze and didn't know what to do. He saw the look of desperation in Jaden's eyes, and that's when Gloria realized he was behind her. His and Jaden's love affair flashed before his eyes and his mind raced through a reel of perfect and beautiful moments. He even saw her holding his unborn child and that's when Ethan knew he had to make a move.

Before even having one thought about it, Ethan lunged forward with his entire body towards Gloria who had since planted the gun right back on Jaden's beautiful face. It all happened so quickly. "Don't, Ethan, or I'll shoot!" were the only words anyone spoken And then one loud bullet shot rang out and the room turned pitch black.

12 FORBIDDEN CONNECTION 3

Journey Into Darkness

As Ethan drove home he was upset with himself for ever doubting Jadan. He couldn't believe the terrible atrocities she had been through. The thought of her living with the memories and the flashbacks of her horrendous ordeal made Ethan feel sick to his stomach and also guilty that he didn't help her more. But he didn't know. She had never revealed these things to him before. God, why hadn't she told him, he thought?

A million questions were running through his mind. If he had only known his second wife had been the victim of such heinous sex crimes, he could have gotten her the help she needed. After all, he is a doctor. His mind was racing. He couldn't wait to get home to his beautiful wife who was now carrying his child. He felt like the luckiest man alive. As Ethan drove up, he noticed the door was ajar. This startled him because Jadan never left a door unlocked! He knew something wasn't right.

He threw the car into park and got out of the car. He raced to the house. He felt that something was terribly wrong as soon as he entered the house. He was shocked by what he saw when he walked into the bedroom. His ex-wife, Gloria, was standing there with a gun to Jadan's head! Without a second thought, Ethan lunged forward. It all happened so quickly.

"Don't Ethan or I'll shoot!" were the only words anyone spoke and then one loud bullet shot rang out and the room went black.

Taken Hostage

Jadan watched as Ethan and Gloria struggled for the gun. Suddenly she was grabbed from behind. A rag was put over her mouth and nose. She was dragged out to the driveway where she was thrown into a car. The car sped away. Ethan and Gloria struggled. Gloria finally gained control of the gun. Ethan lay stunned as Gloria struck him across the brow 3 times with the pistol.

When Ethan finally came to two hours later he woke up groggy as he tried to focus on his surroundings.

"Cat got your tongue Ethan?" said Gloria with an evil tone of voice as she held the pistol pointed straight at Ethan's face. She then broke into a laugh that sounded as if it came straight from hell.

"What is going on?" asked a very confused and shaken up Ethan

Gloria laughed louder as she repeated his words:

"What is going on?" she asked laughing and mocking Ethan's voice.

"You mean you don't know Ethan? I have taken care of things. After all Jadan was a complete embarrassment for you. She was nothing more than a whore and a skank!"

She shrieked with laughter.

Ethan had finally become completely aware of what was going on

"What the fuck did you do with her Gloria? Tell me right now!" he yelled, rubbing his brow.

"Now do you really think I am going to answer that Ethan?"

How did one woman become so dead set on hate and eaten alive with revenge? Ethan couldn't help but wonder this and many other things as well about Gloria.

Ethan stared at her with eyes that burned with pain and fear for Jadan.

"How could you become such an evil monster Gloria? Is this all because I cheated on you years ago? My God you are a sick and twisted bitch!"

"I am sick and twisted alright, you bastard!"

Gloria she held back stinging tears from her eyes. In her mind she had every reason to be angry and vengeful. After all she had adored Ethan and dedicated her whole life to him once upon a time ago.

"Where's Jadan? I demand an answer Gloria!" cried Ethan, struggling with the ropes he was bound in with his hands tied together tightly behind his back.

"Wouldn't you just love to know!" smiled Gloria evilly, still holding back burning tears.

As Jadan came to, she had a raging headache. Her body ached from head to toe. Suddenly her mind raced to Ethan. Oh my God, Ethan! She heard voices all around her. The voices sounded very familiar to her. She recognized the main male voice she heard.

"We did what that bitch Gloria told us to do. She fucking better pay up like she promised or this slut here is dead!"

Jadan closed her eyes pretending to be out of it so she could try and make sense of the turmoil around her. It all started to come back to her. Her mind began to fill with horror. She opened her eyes to a small squint and suddenly realized who the men were. They were her old captors Billy and Johann. They were two of the meanest and most evil men Jadan had ever known. They were the ones who had ruined her life earlier by making her do the heinous things they captured on film. Jadan couldn't believe she was here with these monsters. Her mind raced to Ethan and her unborn child. What on earth was she going to do? She knew she had to hold back the tears that were now stinging her eyes. The longer she pretended to be incoherent the better. This gave her time to consider what to do. She remembered suddenly that the last thing she had heard were gunshots. She also remembered that Ethan's evil ex-wife Gloria was at the heart of this whole nightmare! She couldn't help but wonder, was Ethan still alive? Would she live through this horrific situation?

Fighting the Darkness

Ethan decided that fighting Gloria with bitter words wasn't the answer to this nightmare. He decided that his best bet was to stay quiet and think about how to defeat her. The ropes she had bound him with were stinging his wrists. The knots on his head and brow only seemed to hurt worse as the day moved on. Gloria had left him in the basement of his house tied up on the cold cement floor. He knew she would be back. Waving a gun in his face. He decided he would focus on positive thoughts. Of course his mind raced immediately to his bride Jadan. Was she alive? Had Gloria tied her up somewhere as well? Would their unborn child survive all of this? Ethan felt that Jadan was still alive and that they would survive Gloria's vengeance. He didn't know how or why he thought this, he just simply did. He closed his eyes and let his mind go back to a more peaceful and certainly happier time and place in his life. He remembered his honeymoon night He smiled as his mind went back to that night and all of the romance and passion within it:

Ethan waited anxiously on the bed covered with silk sheets and pillows. The honeymoon suite that he had chosen was romantic. Perfect for his beautiful bride. He had never been as happy as he was at this very moment as he waited for his gorgeous wife to emerge from the bathroom. He felt his cock stiffen underneath the mauve satin sheet as he waited in near torturous anticipation. It felt like his cock would simply explode if she didn't hurry up and make love to him! Then suddenly as if she could sense his thoughts, she emerged looking as breathtaking as Ethan knew she would. She stood there in one spot smiling at Ethan as if to ask his opinion on the beautiful lingerie she was wearing.

"My God, darling you look beautiful beyond words!"

Jadan was wearing a pale pink baby doll set that looked absolutely gorgeous next to her ebony flesh. She chose this particular set because she knew Ethan loved her in this color. He was the most wonderful man she had ever known and now he was her husband. Jadan knew she must be the happiest woman alive!

She smiled and walked over to her new husband on the bed and attacked his body with kisses of luxurious passion. The passion between them was astounding and it had been a part of them ever since the first day they met. As she sat on top of him he slipped her pale pink baby doll top off of her ebony shoulders and kissed them. Jadan could feel his hard girth pressing against her, feeling as if it was in dire need of being deep inside of her hot velvet tunnel of love. She guided his hard cock inside of her and rode him with a vehement passion she had never had before. She loved Ethan so much and he adored her as well. He never realized that love and sex could be this wonderful. His first marriage had been a nightmare.

Ethan grabbed Jadan's luscious ass cheeks in his hands and squeezed her tighter into him and harder down onto his throbbing meat. He *had never been made love to her as passionately as he was right now. As she rode him hard he watched her hot tits bounce up and down. He had always been incredibly turned on by her huge nipples. They were almost burgundy in color and they set his cock on fire every time he looked at them. He reached up and twisted them between his thumb and index fingers and she purred in red hot pleasure.*

He could feel her cunt tightening around his iron hard cock. Her lips sucked him in tighter and tighter as she fucked him furiously now! Her moves upon his stiff prick were as ferocious as always been. Ethan loved how she fucked him.

After Jadan rode his cock he mounted her in the missionary position. He slipped his wet cock inside of her gently and lovingly. Jadan moaned a softly and held his face in her hands. They kissed as their bodies melted into one. They came in a mutual orgasm that truly seemed to stop time and space. It set their love in stone forever.

Ethan smiled to himself. He knew that time was of the essence to find her. He didn't really know how. He knew deep in his heart his wife was alive and he also knew he would find her if it killed him!

He heard footsteps coming and he assumed it was the evil bitch, his ex-wife Gloria. He had to find a way to get loose and get the gun away from her before it was too late. He decided he would play along with her for now to keep her anger to a minimum. The calmer Gloria remained the better as far as he was concerned.

"Hello Ethan how are you doing this evening?" Gloria said in an unusually calm and extremely eerie tone of voice.

Ethan refused to speak. He simply shrugged his shoulders.

Gloria acted out in anger and hit him across the head with the butt end of her pistol. Ethan winced in pain but refused to let Gloria see how badly it hurt him.

"What the fuck is wrong with you, you son of a bitch? You will fucking speak when I ask you a question you good for nothing bastard!"

She yelled and kicked him hard in the shin with her high heel shoe.

"What is it you want me to say darling?"

Ethan feigned care and concern in his voice.

"Gloria I realize now that you are right dear. I should have NEVER cheated on you. I am so sorry darling will you forgive me and stop this charade?"

Gloria looked at him with a puzzled expression in her glassed over eyes. She was so eaten up with revenge and hatred it manifested throughout her whole body from head to toe. Her face had a wrinkled and distorted appearance and she looked older than her age of 40. Ethan truly wondered what on earth he ever saw in this conniving and good for nothing woman standing before him. He did, however, know what he saw in his Jadan and there was absolutely NOTHING he wouldn't do to be reunited with her once and for all. He was even willing to fake care and concern for Gloria if that's what it took and Ethan had a sneaking suspicion it would take that and then some. He wondered just how far he would have to go.

Billy walked over to Jadan who was still feigning being knocked unconscious, but by this time Billy wasn't buying her act one bit. He yelled into her face

"Wake up Jadan, you slut!"

Jadan could smell his rancid breath and it made her stomach turn. Jadan slowly opened her eyes and could see Billy's disgusting grin over her. It took her back 6 years earlier when he had forced her to do such vile acts. Jadan couldn't believe that here she was thrust back into this evil life with these two losers Billy and his stupid sidekick Johann,

"So Jadan are you excited about filming part two of "Destination Humiliation?"

The very thought of it made Jadan nearly physically ill as she held back the lump forming in her throat.

"Frankly I don't care if you're excited or not. Get ready to show the rest of the world how filthy you can be."

He chuckled. Johann joined in as they chided Jadan and both grabbed a tit and squeezed as if to tantalize her even more.

Jadan was holding back stinging tears forming in her ebony colored eyes. She missed her husband, Ethan so badly. She wondered if he was even still alive. She remembered the revenge that was dead set on his ex-wife's Gloria's face. To keep herself from going insane, Jadan let her mind drift off to a better place. She suddenly began to think about the time she and Ethan first made love on the beach the only way she could find to exist within the horror she had found herself in was to think back:

She and Ethan had just arrived on the island. Ethan had never been out of the states before so Jadan was excited to show him her old stomping grounds. On their first evening out on the island she decided to take him to her favorite private oasis, a secluded beach that was brimming with romance and beauty all around. One could almost picture former days with a pirate ship quietly anchored in the secluded, protective cove while the pirates drank their grog on shore by a blazing fire chasing half naked native women around with hard-ons from spending too much time at sea. Jadan loved coming to this private cove as a girl to unwind and relax and she was very thrilled to be taking Ethan to see it now. They got there just about the time of sunset. The sky was ablaze with colors of red, mauves and burnt sienna. Ethan's eyes were twinkling in the setting sun as Jadan wrapped her arms around his neck for a warm kiss. The simple kiss quickly turned into a hot kiss that led the two of them down to the sand. Jadan laid a blanket out for them as they heard the waves crashing to shore. The sound of the water had always been a source of relaxation for Jadan, and now as she lay in the arms of her true love it truly sent her to paradise.

Jadan kissed Ethan with a vehement rapture and the waves seemed to be in rhythm with their bodies as they undulated up and down prepared to make sweet love. The combination of love and hot lust was something

Jadan loved most about their relationship. They had always found the perfect balance between lovemaking and all out lusty sex that sent their bodies to another place. Jadan's favorite way to fuck Ethan was her on top riding his massive meat to the point of mutual orgasms.

She did her usual moves atop his throbbing hard on and swirled her hips in figure eights around his boner. Ethan growled a deep chesty groan as he felt her pussy lips tighten around his aching shaft. Jadan winced in delight as she purposely squeezed her lips as hard as she could around his hard muscle. She knew Ethan went wild when she did this. He grabbed her ass hard and yanked her down as hard as he could upon his stiff prick. He thrust upwards as stiffly as he could as well to bury his meat as deep inside as he could get it.

Jadan knew she felt an orgasm coming but she wasn't quite ready to give it up just yet. So she suddenly decided to go down on his cock with her mouth. As she did she could taste her own sweet pussy on it and it turned her on even more. If Jadan tasted her own juices on Ethan it made her even hornier and more amorous to make Ethan and her shoot off. She sucked him right up until the point she knew he was about to gush all over her mouth and down her hot throat. Then she stopped and mounted his hard cock once more. She rode him passionately with love and just the right amount of lust. They began to cum at precisely the same time as their bodies melted into one seething hot body of sheer romance and passion.

Suddenly Jadan was startled back to reality by a brash voice.

"Hey baby, wake up it's time for you to get to work." screamed Johann, Billy's cohort, right in Jadan's face. Jadan looked at Johann

"Why the confused look baby?" asked Johann while he reached out to stroke Jadan's pretty face. Jadan couldn't help it. She got so mad that she spit right in his face making Johann livid. She doesn't remember much after that. Everything went black again.

The Long Road Back

Ethan spent hours trying to loosen the ropes around his wrists. He was making progress. He knew how long Gloria would be gone and approximately how long he had to work on his wrists and trying to get free. He had a pounding headache from the hits to the head he had endured all due to Gloria and the butt end of her pistol. He had no idea if Jadan was even alive but he refused to give up. His gut told him she was very much alive and needed him desperately. He hoped his gut feelings were right this time. Ethan knew he only had maybe 2 more hours at the most to loosen his ropes. He was trying every technique he had ever learned from the Navy, He knew one day those tricks he learned with knots might come in handy. This was a time to recall them if there ever was a time. Ethan worked diligently for what seemed like days until he got it loose! He crawled his way over to the metal edge of a pipe in the basement and rubbed one side of the rope on one wrist against it time and time again until he thought he might pass out from sheer exhaustion.

His diligence was well worth it in the end. He had managed to get the ropes off. Now he had only 30 minutes at the most to position himself behind the door. He knew he had only one chance to contain her. He couldn't knock her out completely if he wanted to find out where Jadan was. Unbeknownst to Gloria, He kept a pistol in the basement, so he grabbed it and got ready for her return.

Jadan finally started to come around after being hit hard in the head. She began to get her bearings and remembered what had happened. She spit in Johann's face and he didn't like it too. Then Jadan remembered black darkness once again that overtook her, and now the pain she suffered was the proof of another hit to her head.

She had no idea what she was going to do or how she was going to get away but she knew she had better start making a plan before it was too late. She didn't even want to think about the movies and photos that she had taken part in years earlier. The memories of it all were simply too painful for her to think of. It was humiliating and painful. There was no way she could even think about it yet alone relive the horrid memories. All that she could think of was Ethan, the man she loved and adored, the man who had taken her life and given it new meaning. Now she carried his child. Would she make it away from these monsters, Billy and Johann before it was too late? Would her unborn child live to meet his mom and dad? These were the questions that plagued her mind. She drifted off back into darkness and dreamed of her beloved Ethan.

Ethan heard Gloria's car outside in the driveway and he felt his heart hammering away in his chest. He hoped he could pull this off. He truly hoped for his sake, and Jadan's that he could. He knew he would have to act fast to contain Gloria and find out the information that he needed to find out to save his wife in time. His heart pounded so loud, he was in fear Gloria might hear it at the top of the stairs. With each click of her high heels on the old cement steps, Ethan's breathing increased more and more. By the time she made it to the last one and put her hand on the doorknob Ethan thought he might have a massive heart attack right there on the spot. Gloria turned the doorknob and Ethan prepared to tackle her to the ground as she walked past him. He knew he couldn't make one false move or it would be all over for Jadan. He just hoped and prayed he wasn't too late to save his wife. When Gloria emerged through the doorway Ethan moved fast and as stealthily as a ninja. He tackled her to the floor in one move and was able to wrestle her gun from her before she fired a shot right into his temple. In fact Ethan moved to perfectly in time that Gloria's face had a look of horror on it as he now controlled her as opposed to her controlling him. Gloria crawled backwards along the dirty basement concrete begging Ethan not to shoot her.

"I am not going to shoot you Gloria. I considered it but then I thought why go to prison for the rest of my life over a bitch like you!" Ethan replied in hot anger. "On top if that if I killed you I wouldn't find out where Jadan was now would I?" he said as he held the pistol pointing right at Gloria's bitter and now ugly face.

"You are going to tell me what you did with my wife who by the way is carrying my child and you are going to tell me now!" growled Ethan in a voice that would cut through stone. "If she dies you will have two murders on your hands Gloria. Is that what you want you evil cunt?"

Gloria was shaking uncontrollably by now and hot tears once again formed in her black eyes. "Okay Okay! I will tell you Ethan where your little slut Jadan is! Please just put the gun away!" she cried uncontrollably.

"I ought to kill you right now you vile bitch!" Ethan growled again almost unable to control himself from pulling the pistol's trigger.

"Tell me where she is Gloria!!" he demanded "Tell me right fucking now!"

"The little skank is with her old kidnappers Billy and Johann out on old highway 54 on the outskirts of town!" she yelled "I hope they haven't hurt the little whore yet though" she said with yet another evil grin across her wretched face.

Ethan's finger wanted so badly to pull the trigger and blow this cunt away but he knew it wasn't in him to end lives. He was a surgeon he was in the business of saving lives. Instead Ethan called the police who quickly made it to the house and put Gloria in cuffs and headed to the station to print and book her for the many counts of felonies she had facing her.

Ethan got in the car with two of the toughest detectives in town headed for the outskirts of town to a seedy motel called the "Stay and Go." Gloria had told him it was room 66 they were staying in. God he just hoped he made it to his darling Jadan in time before the worst had happened.

The cop car pulled into the driveway of the motel. The cops got their guns ready to storm the room. They eased up to the doorway and could hear voices. Ethan could see his wife inside moving around which told him she was alive! The next few minutes were a blur. . It took a few bullets, but both of the losers but they went down big time and were cuffed and carried off in the cop car. Ethan and Jadan embraced. He never intended on letting his precious wife out of his sight again. The two of them headed to the hospital to get checked out. They both got a clean bill of health aside from a few bruises and scratches. The baby was fine too! They were both ecstatic to hear that news. It took a few weeks of recuperation but Ethan and Jadan were finally well and whole again.

Reunited

It had been a while since they had enjoyed each other sexually so Jadan planned a reunion like no other chock full of candles and romance. When Ethan came home that night from the clinic he was beside himself at all the trouble his wife had gone through.

After a meal of all of his favorite foods he and Jadan retired to their bedroom where she began kissing him with the passion that made him fall in love with her in the first place. She mounted his cock once again and rode him like she had never ridden his cock before. She sat straight up on it and moved her hips slowly one way and then the other being sure to take in all of his amazing length and girth. He groaned in red hot pleasure as he felt her pussy contract around his swelling member. He had never felt her pussy so horny or so greedy for him in all of their time of fucking and making love. She felt amazing inside, and his cock never felt as good as it did right then and there.

It didn't take much of Jadan riding his cock before the two of them exploded in an orgasm that seemed to last for hours as opposed to moments. She sat down as hard as she could and threw her head back as her hot cunt came all over Ethan covering him in her hot juices. His dick got as hard as steel and unloaded what seemed like a gallon of cum inside of his beautiful wife. They collapsed in each other's arms knowing that they would never part. Ethan had no intention of ever letting her go again. He adored Jadan and she him.

Six short months later Jadan gave birth to their first child. She had a beautiful baby girl that had her ebony skin color and Ethan's black curls. They named her Destiny Cherish to commemorate the love they shared for one another. They were the happiest couple that either of them could imagine had ever existed and their baby girl Destiny only sealed that.

The End

AUTHOR'S NOTE

Readers: I want to expand a few of the stories to see where the characters can be explored further. If there are any of the stories that you would like to read more about again, I'd love to hear from you!

Visit my blog at www.tenaseldan.com

Join my newsletter for free exclusive previews www.tenaseldan.com/in

Follow me on Twitter at www.twitter.com/tenaseldan

Like my page on Facebook at www.facebook.com/tenaseldan

Discover my books at major ebook retailers everywhere.